"You don't have to put on an act for me.

"You've been through a lot. It's okay to be vulnerable. You may be a police officer, but you're also human. I'll do everything in my power to help you. I'll stay with you if that's what it takes to make sure you feel secure."

Nia blew a sigh. Her body shifted as she looked him in the eyes. "Thank you, Drew. Honestly? I am still a little shaken up. I don't even go into the kitchen to get a glass of water without taking my gun with me. But I'm working through it. And the camera your friend installed has helped ease my anxiety, too, so..."

"So, you're hanging in there?"

"Yes. I'm hanging in there." Her lips spread into a faint smile. "I appreciate you looking out for me."

Drew's chest pulled at her gratitude. It was confirmation that his words of encouragement were well received. Nia's response deepened his need to protect her, triggering a surge of emotions that fueled his burgeoning attraction.

T0205133

HOMETOWN HOMICIDE

DENISE N. WHEATLEY

INTRIGUE

To my aunts, Sharon and Glenda. I love you!

Harlequin®
INTRIGUE™

Recycling programs
for this product may
not exist in your area.

ISBN-13: 978-1-335-45695-3

Hometown Homicide

Copyright © 2024 by Denise N. Wheatley

Harlequin Enterprises ULC
22 Adelaide St. West, 41st Floor
Toronto, Ontario M5H 4E3, Canada
www.Harlequin.com

Printed in Lithuania

MIX
Paper | Supporting
responsible forestry
FSC® C021394

Denise N. Wheatley loves happy endings and the art of storytelling. Her novels run the romance gamut, and she strives to pen entertaining books that embody matters of the heart. She's an RWA member and holds a BA in English from the University of Illinois. When Denise isn't writing, she enjoys watching true-crime TV and chatting with readers. Follow her on social media.

Instagram: @Denise_Wheatley_Writer
Twitter: @DeniseWheatley
BookBub: @DeniseNWheatley
Goodreads: Denise N. Wheatley

Books by Denise N. Wheatley

Harlequin Intrigue

A West Coast Crime Story

The Heart-Shaped Murders
Danger in the Nevada Desert
Homicide at Vincent Vineyard
Hometown Homicide

An Unsolved Mystery Book

Cold Case True Crime

Bayou Christmas Disappearance
Backcountry Cover-Up

Harlequin Medical Romance

ER Doc's Las Vegas Reunion

Visit the Author Profile page at Harlequin.com.

CAST OF CHARACTERS

Nia Brooks—An ambitious former 9-1-1 operator turned rookie police officer in small-town Juniper, Colorado.

Drew Taylor—A ten-year veteran Juniper police officer.

Ivy Brooks—Nia's younger sister, who is considered the black sheep of the family.

Bruce Mitchell—Juniper PD's chief of police.

Officer Martin Davis—A rambunctious Juniper police officer.

Shane Anderson—Juniper's newest bachelor, who has his eye on Nia.

Ethan Rogers—A prominent businessman who is a member of Legacy, a prestigious men's social club.

Vaughn Clayton—An attorney running for senator and who is also a member of Legacy.

Prologue

"9-1-1. What is your emergency?"

"Someone's trying to break into my house!" a woman screeched into the phone.

Operator Nia Brooks shot straight up in her chair. The buzz within Juniper, Colorado's communications center was louder than normal as the phone lines had been dead for hours. Increasing the volume on her headset, she scanned the computer screen for the caller's location.

"What is your address, ma'am?"

"Three eighty-two Barksdale Road."

"And you said that someone is trying to break into your house?"

"*Yes.* A man has been banging on the back door and fighting with the knob for several minutes now. I'm here alone, and…"

The woman fell silent. A loud thud penetrated Nia's eardrums, followed by a deep, muffled howl.

"Do you *hear* him?" the woman hissed.

"I do," Nia replied, forcing a calm tone as her fingers flew across the keyboard. "I'm already in contact with the police dispatcher alerting them to the situation. Law enforcement should be heading your way. Just stay on the line with me—"

"*Listen,*" the woman interrupted, her voice breaking into

a jagged whisper. "I told you I'm here by myself. I don't have any weapons. If this maniac makes his way inside my house, I have no way of protecting myself. So *please* tell the authorities to hurry up!"

She paused at what sounded like a bat pounding the door.

"Leave me alone!" the woman screamed. "I'm on the phone with 9-1-1 and police are on their way!"

"Yes, they are," Nia assured her. "I can see that law enforcement is en route to your house. And they're aware that this is a high-priority emergency situation."

Quivering sobs rattled Nia's headset as the woman whimpered, "They need to hurry up and get here. This man is about to break down the door. When he does, he might try to kill me!"

"Are all of your windows and doors locked?"

"I think so—yes. I turned off all the lights, too, hoping that would somehow run him off. Obviously it didn't work."

"Well, the secured windows and doors should keep him at bay until police arrive. In the meantime, I'll be right here on the line with you. What is your name, ma'am?"

"Linda. Linda Echols."

"Okay, Linda. When the knocking first began, did you happen to take a look outside and get a glimpse of the man?"

The woman paused, only the sound of her unsteady breaths swooshing through Nia's headset. "I—I did. Just once. When the banging started. I looked out to see what all the commotion was about and tried to tell him that he had the wrong house, not realizing he was trying to break in. He insisted that he was exactly where he was supposed to be. But he's dressed in all black and looks to be wearing a mask and—*wait!* I think he might be..."

She went silent again.

"Linda, talk to me. Tell me what's going on. I don't hear anything."

"Yeah, neither do I. Maybe he finally decided to stop—"

Boom, boom, boom!

Nia cringed at the rapid succession of thumping.

"Linda?"

Silence.

"Linda! Are you okay? What is he doing now?"

"He just picked up one of my patio chairs and is slamming it against the window! He's gonna break it and get inside. I need for the police to get here. *Now!*"

Just as Nia enlarged the map on her screen and checked the responding officer's location, a message from dispatch flashed below it.

Inform the caller that police are on the way, but due to construction they've been rerouted, causing a delay.

Clenching her teeth, a frustrated grunt gurgled in Nia's throat. This was the hard part of the job—the part that she couldn't control. It pained her, being on the front line with the victims from behind a desk as opposed to in person.

"Where are the cops?" Linda rasped. "Are they almost here?"

"They're still on the way. But there's roadwork near your home that's blocking the direct route. So as soon as they get around that they'll arrive at your house. And like I said, I'll be right here with you until they—"

Crack!

Nia jerked in her chair as the sound of shattering glass pierced her ears, followed by Linda's guttural scream.

"He's getting in!"

Inhaling sharply, Nia asked, "He's getting inside the house?"

"Yes! He just smashed the sliding glass door!"

Nia pounded the keyboard with an update to dispatch while clambering footsteps stuttered through her headset.

"I'm still here with you, Linda. What's happening now?"

"I'm running upstairs to hide inside my bedroom closet. *Please* tell the cops to hurry up and get here!"

A faint shuffling echoed in the background.

"He's inside the house!" Linda whisper-screamed as the sound of shoe soles squeaked across the floor.

"Hey!" a gravelly voice roared. "Get your ass back down here!"

"Linda," Nia began, struggling to maintain her composure, "are you inside the bedroom yet?"

"I am now."

"Good. Make sure you lock the door. Can you push a dresser or a chair or some sort of heavy object in front of it?"

"I can try, but I don't think I can move this chest of drawers across the carpet!"

Eyeing the map on her screen, Nia checked the responding officer's location. Her chest tightened at the sight of the vehicle's marker. It was at a standstill.

The intruder's demands boomed in the distance, followed by Linda's hysterical cries.

Bam!

"He's forcing his way inside the bedroom!"

A throbbing pain pulsated over Nia's left eye. She pounded her fist against the desk, watching helplessly as the responding officer's vehicle finally began to move.

"Linda, the police are making their way to your house. Is there anywhere inside the bedroom you can hide? The closet? Or bathroom?"

The other end of the call went silent.

"Hello?" Nia called out. "Hello! Are you still there?"

"I'm gonna kill you," she heard a man grunt.

"*Linda!*"

A jarring thump preceded heaving gasps.

"I'm gonna kill you," the man muttered again over the sound of gut-wrenching gurgling.

Nia's body weakened at the thought of Linda being killed.

Come on! she wanted to scream after seeing that police were still several blocks away from the victim's house.

Just as she typed another message to dispatch alerting them to the severity of the situation, the call dropped.

Chapter One

Officer Drew Taylor kicked in the cracked wooden panels hanging from the door of Shelby's Candy Factory before stepping inside. The place had been closed for years and sat abandoned on the land bordering Juniper and Finchport. Since it was in Juniper's jurisdiction, the town had made plans to demolish the property last year and build affordable housing in its place. But then protestors had stepped in, insisting that the historic landmark merited preservation.

The powers that be agreed to halt demolition after activists promised to renovate the building. Their plan to turn it into a multipurpose community center, however, had yet to happen after fundraising efforts failed. In the meantime, the factory remained vacant—and dangerous.

Teens had been using the space to throw wild parties while squatters saw it as a place to hang out, drink and sleep for days on end. Law enforcement did their best to keep out the riffraff. But the moment they drove away, loiterers and partygoers sneaked right back onto the scene.

Shelby's had become a point of contention for most Juniper residents. The quaint town of just over 10,000, located right outside Denver, prided itself on a welcoming spirit, solid family values, neighborly kindness and tight-knit bonds. Many of the cafés, boutiques and service businesses had been passed down from generation to generation. The hardworking community strove to maintain a glowing reputation, which was vital considering many of Denver's tourism dollars trickled over into Juniper's agricultural museum, vintage car shows and antique mall.

Most residents felt as though Shelby's had become a stain on the town. Nothing good had come of allowing it to remain standing—especially now, as Drew had been called there to investigate a dead body.

He and his partner, Timothy Braxton, walked across the dilapidated main level in search of the crime scene. Layers of dust covered the 3,000 square feet of cracked cement flooring. Shards of glass were scattered everywhere as large holes marred the cloudy picture windows. Pulleys once used to lift heavy candy-filled cauldrons were still in place, as were a few of the cooling tables and taffy-spinning machines.

"Officers, over here!"

Drew and Timothy made their way past a row of drop roller machines toward the back of the factory. The stench of decomposing flesh hit before Drew even laid eyes on the victim.

"Oh my God…" Timothy uttered, holding his hand to his nose.

A deceased woman's body sat propped up in a metal folding chair. She'd been bound and gagged. Dried blood had pooled around her neck and chest.

Drew's stomach lurched at the sight. Juniper rarely saw crimes this brutal. Thefts, drug deals and bar fights were the norm—not vicious murders committed by demented killers, who, the officer feared, would kill again.

The victim looked to be in her mid to late twenties. Five foot six if he had to guess, and about 135 pounds minus the postmortem bloating. Her long, dark brown hair was a tangled mess. If he hadn't seen the back of her white T-shirt, he would've thought it was a reddish brown as the front had been completely soaked in blood. Layers of duct tape were wrapped around her wrists and ankles. While her dark blue jeans appeared to be intact, she wasn't wearing any shoes.

"Any word on who the victim is?" Drew asked Officer Davis.

"Yep. Her name is Katie Douglas."

"So she had ID on her?"

"No. When the call came in over the radio that a body had been found, whoever tipped off law enforcement knew the victim but asked to remain anonymous."

Drew bent down and studied the woman's skin. Judging by the green discoloration, along with the mixture of blood and foam leaking from her mouth, she'd been dead for a few days.

He pulled a handkerchief from the pocket of his black cargo pants and waved off several blowflies before holding it to his nose. "Have you found any evidence that might contain DNA?"

Officer Davis held a brown paper bag in the air with a gloved hand. "So far, just a piece of duct tape with a bloody fingerprint that I spotted near the victim's feet."

"Good. Let's make sure we get that sent off to the crime lab as soon as possible."

"Will do. Oh, and there was one more thing…"

The officer handed over a brochure. Drew slipped on a pair of latex gloves before taking it. "What is this?"

"An event calendar for Latimer Park's recreational center. We found it stuffed inside the victim's hand."

"Hmm, interesting…"

In between the blood stains, Drew studied the activity

details. There was a wide variety of them, from pumpkin-carving contests to crafting classes. "I wonder if she's somehow affiliated with the park. But I don't see her name listed as an instructor or host on any of the events."

Peering over his shoulder, Timothy asked, "Are there any handwritten notes on it? Or phone numbers?"

"Nope. Nothing. We'll send this to the lab as well. See what DNA might be detected. We should also stop by Latimer Park and pick up a calendar on the way back to the station. I wanna have that on hand just in case we can somehow trace the victim to the park."

Drew made his way toward the back wall. A door that was normally boarded up had been yanked from the hinges. "Hey, Davis, where's the forensic team?"

"They're on the way."

"And the medical examiner?"

"She's at the hospital wrapping up an autopsy. She should be here soon."

"Can you let me know when she arrives? I'd like to speak with her."

Officer Davis's eyelids lowered, as if he wanted to question Drew. Instead he replied, "Uh...yeah. Sure."

Ignoring his confusion, Drew pulled out his cell phone and took several photos of the scene. After nearly ten years on the force, his colleagues still didn't seem to understand his behavior once he slipped into investigative mode. Drew had a habit of taking over, oftentimes making a list of duties for his fellow officers while collecting forensic evidence on his own. Today would be no different.

As he began filming a video, Drew contemplated what the victim had gone through before being murdered. Had she been drugged and kidnapped? Did she know her killer? Was it someone she'd trusted?

He squeezed his eyes shut, thinking of how this could have been someone he knew. The thought sent a streak of anger through his chest that pushed past his lungs and out his mouth in the form of a loud grunt.

"You all right?" Timothy asked, following him into the alleyway behind the building.

"No. I'm not. I've gotta do something here. As a matter of fact, I don't wanna wait on the forensic team. I've got my kit in the trunk of the car. I'll let the medical examiner handle the processing of the body while I collect whatever evidence I can find. Fingerprints, shoe prints, blood trails—anything I can get my hands on. I've got a bad feeling about this one, Tim. If we don't catch the suspect soon, trust me, he *will* kill again."

DREW STOOD OUTSIDE Chief Mitchell's door gnawing at his bottom lip. The chief never called him to his office. At least not for a one-on-one meeting. Usually when he wanted to talk he'd call Timothy in with him. This time, he specifically asked to speak to Drew alone.

Just as he raised his fist to knock, the door flew open. Officer Davis came charging out.

"Hey, man!" he said, giving Drew a hearty slap on the back. "Listen, great job at the crime scene today. Way to step up and take the lead. Oh, and congrats!"

"Thanks. But wait, congrats on what?"

"The chief will tell you. I'm late for an appointment. Let's catch up tomorrow!"

Remaining planted in the doorway, Drew's brows furrowed as the officer darted down the hallway.

"Hey, Taylor!" Chief Mitchell called out. "Come on in. That damn Davis has such a big mouth. He never could hold water, could he?"

"Not since I've met him, sir, which was during our days at the academy. But what is he supposed to be keeping from me?"

"Close the door and have a seat. That's what I need to talk to you about."

Drew made his way inside the cluttered office. While pulling out a worn burgundy tweed chair, he eyed the cardboard boxes stacked against the empty filing cabinets. Framed pictures and certificates that had yet to be hung were propped against the wall. Containers of unopened supplies hugged the side of his desk. No one would know the chief had taken over the space almost thirty years ago considering it looked as if he'd just moved in.

"So," Chief Mitchell began, his chubby jowls quivering, "Officer Davis just updated me on the crime scene at Shelby's. Such a shame, finding Katie like that. Poor girl…"

"Sir, are you okay?" Drew asked after the chief's voice broke.

"Yeah, yeah. I'm good. I went to high school with the victim's father. So I feel somewhat connected to this case. Her dad called me this afternoon and the man was inconsolable. I promised him we'd do everything in our power to catch the sick son of a bitch who did this to his daughter. Which is where you come in, Officer Taylor."

Drew nodded, his eyes drifting toward the stack of boxes sitting directly behind the chief. The one on top caught his attention. "Linda Echols" was scribbled across the side in bold black letters.

It had been almost a year since her murder occurred, leading to one of the toughest investigations Drew had ever worked. No viable evidence was found at the scene of her home invasion. With the house being in an isolated area, no witnesses came forward and no security footage surfaced. Every lead hit a dead end. Eventually, the case went cold.

Since Linda's death, not a day had gone by that Drew didn't think about it. He'd grown extremely close to her family while working the investigation. After speaking to Linda's mother on an almost daily basis, he made a promise to catch her killer. When that didn't happen, he'd considered quitting the force. But it was Chief Mitchell who had encouraged him to remain onboard.

"You'll never make an arrest if you're no longer a member of Juniper PD," the chief told him. When Drew expressed feeling like a failure after making a promise he couldn't keep, his boss stopped him. "Listen, son. This was your first lesson in understanding that sometimes, working in the field of criminal justice means playing the long game. Hell, some cold cases don't get solved until twenty or thirty years down the road. But the key is, if you work hard enough, they eventually will. So keep your head up and hang in there."

Those were the words that kept Drew on the force, prompting him to pin a photo of Linda inside his cubicle as a reminder to never give up on trying to solve her case. And now, after hanging a picture of Katie next to hers, Drew hoped the investigation would somehow come full circle and lead him to Linda's killer. He had to consider the possibility of the cases being connected, considering both women's throats had been slashed and Linda's attacker was still on the loose.

"Well," Chief Mitchell said, pulling Drew from his thoughts, "let's talk about why I asked to meet with you. When Officer Davis and I were discussing the crime scene, he mentioned how you really stepped up and took on a leadership role with getting the reports completed, holding critical conversations with the medical examiner and forensic team, and gathering evidence. Then of course there were the photos and videos you captured… Keep this up and you'll be stepping into my shoes once I finally decide to retire."

"*Wow*. That's, uh…that's quite the compliment coming from you, Chief. Thank you."

"Of course. It's a compliment well-earned. And the reason I'm saying all that is because I'd like for you to head up the Katie Douglas murder investigation."

Drew sat straight up, turning his ear in the chief's direction. "I'm sorry. I think I misheard you. What did you just say?"

"I said I'd like for you to be the lead investigator on the Douglas case."

The weight of the request sent him slumping in his chair. Hundreds of thoughts flew through Drew's mind. There were at least three other officers who were more qualified than him. Officers who'd been with the Juniper PD way longer and weren't still carrying the burden of Linda Echols's cold case.

"I—I don't know what to say," he stammered. "This is such a huge investigation, and—"

"Wait, are you saying that you don't want to take this on?"

"No, no. It's not that. I'm just thinking about all the other officers who have more seniority than I do. Like Nelson or Harper or Adams—"

"Officer Taylor. I'm asking *you*. Davis wasn't the only one who came to me with great feedback on the way you handled that crime scene today. I received calls from the medical examiner and head of forensics. They both sang your praises. Not Nelson's, Harper's, or Adam's. Nor anybody else's on the homicide team. *Yours*."

Pulling in a puff of air, Drew leaned back, his eyes glazing over as he stared into the speckled drop ceiling. Moments like this were the reason he'd joined the force. This was his time—his opportunity to prove he was capable of getting a murder solved.

"So what do you say, Officer Taylor. Are you in?"

Gripping the arms on his chair, Drew slid to the edge and looked Chief Mitchell directly in the eyes.

"Absolutely, sir. I'm in."

Chapter Two

Nia pulled a mirror from her drawer and checked her reflection. The beach waves she'd carefully flat-ironed through her long chocolate brown bob that morning were still intact. But her T-zone was shiny and lip gloss had faded.

Glancing at the time on her laptop screen, she saw that the special officers' meeting called by Chief Mitchell was set to begin in ten minutes.

"Just enough time to freshen up," she muttered, grabbing her makeup bag and swiping powder across her nose and gloss over her lips.

A knock against her cubicle's frame sent her jumping in her chair.

"Good morning, Officer Brooks."

Nia spun around, rolling her eyes at her smirking work bestie and former 9-1-1 colleague, Cynthia Lee. The pair had grown close while working together in the emergency services department. After Linda Echols's devastating murder last year, Nia was hit with the desire to serve a bigger purpose. Within days she submitted a transfer, and with Chief Mitchell's blessing, joined the police academy.

"Good morning, Cyn. What are you doing away from the call center this early?"

"Well, I've been here since five this morning. So I'm on my break. But here's a better question. What's with the flowing curls and face full of makeup? You got a hot date or something?"

"*Please*. Don't start with me. I'm just making sure I look presentable for the officers' meeting."

"Yeah, right. Presentable would've been a neat pony-tail and dab of lip balm, like *I* normally wear," Cynthia quipped, propping her hands underneath her cherubic freckled face. "But you look like you're getting ready for a photo shoot. It's not like you even need all that with your gorgeous skin, those modelesque cheekbones and incessant gym visits. I mean, you keep the men's heads turning around here." She paused, glancing over her shoulder before whispering, "Could all the primping have anything to do with *Drew*?"

Nia grabbed her arm and pulled her farther inside the cubicle. "Will you lower your voice? Better yet, cut that talk out altogether. You know I'm not into Drew like that."

"Oh, do I really? Because last time I checked, you've been pining after that man ever since you started working for Juniper PD."

"*Lies,*" Nia rebutted, checking her reflection one last time before slapping her compact shut. "Now I may have mentioned that Drew is a handsome guy—"

"Juniper's very own Boris Kodjoe to be exact."

"But you know my rule. I don't date coworkers. Plus Drew seems like such a grump. Like he's always in a bad mood. Not to mention he's never paid an ounce of attention to me."

"First of all, most people meet their partners at work, so you need to toss that rule out the window. Secondly, how would Drew even know you're interested in him? It's not like you've ever gone out of your way to talk to him. Or say hello even."

"Isn't your break over yet?" Nia asked, pushing away from the desk.

"Nope. I've still got five minutes left."

"Well, I need to get to the conference room. So we'll have to table this conversation for later. Or better yet, just forget about it."

"Look," Cynthia said, stopping Nia before she brushed past her. "Do me a favor. At least try and sit next to Drew during this meeting. Maybe start up a conversation. Say good morning. *Something.*"

"Enjoy the rest of your morning, Cynthia," Nia retorted before rushing down the hallway.

"Hey! Are we still on for lunch?"

"Yes, see you at noon!"

The conversation was out of Nia's head before she reached the conference room. All eyes were on her when she walked through the door. Gripping her notebook tighter, she ducked her head while searching for an empty chair.

The majority of the other officers were already there—including Drew. Cynthia hadn't been totally wrong in her assessment of Nia's feelings for him. She had been crushing on the officer ever since her first day of work. Aside from his ruggedly handsome good looks, there was a kindness behind his brooding, intense gaze. Drew was popular among their peers, oftentimes managing to drum up a few laughs despite his no-nonsense attitude. That, along with his impressive career accomplishments, made him one of the most well-respected officers within the department.

But Nia never allowed her crush to go too far. And while she had no intention of breaking her "no dating colleagues" policy, it wasn't as if he was available anyway. Rumor had it he'd been seeing someone for years.

Tables for two were set up alongside the conference room

walls. The only empty space left was directly behind Drew. Just as he glanced in her direction, Nia dropped her gaze to the floor. Her calf muscles burned as she rushed past him and plopped down into the chair. Hoping he hadn't seen her ogling him, she flipped to an empty page in her notebook, then nervously bounced her pen against the table.

Drew turned slightly. He didn't look directly at her, but judging by the curl in his downturned lips, something was annoying him.

The pen, she thought. *Stop banging the pen!*

The second Nia's hand froze midtap, Drew turned back around and faced the front of the room.

Her jaws clenched with embarrassment while he proceeded to talk to his partner, Timothy. When he spoke, the indentations in his biceps flexed as he waved an arm in the air. Tim's jokes sent him twisting in his chair, those gleaming white teeth lighting up the entire area. Nia's lips parted after he ran his strong, nimble hands over his freshly cut hair. She couldn't help but wonder what they'd feel like pressed against her body.

Just as her thoughts trickled from her head down to her tingling chest, a commotion erupted near the doorway. The room grew silent when Chief Mitchell approached the podium.

"Good morning, everyone. I'm sure you're wondering why I called this meeting on such short notice. But don't worry. I'll get right to it, then let you go as we've got a lot of work to do. I recently received a call from Finchport PD's chief of police, and he was telling me about a mentoring program that he's implemented within the department."

"Ugh," Drew grunted, slumping against the wall. "Here we go. Something else to add to my plate that I don't have time for…"

When a series of groans rippled through the room, the chief held up his hand. "Hold on. Before you all go shooting down my idea, just hear me out. I know we're all busy, but none of us are too busy to help out a fellow officer. Now, Finchport's chief has partnered his veteran officers with rookie cops in order to help them adjust to working on the force. As many of you know, being out on the street feels a lot different than training in the academy."

Drew leaned toward Timothy, whispering, "If anybody on this force can't navigate the streets of Juniper, then they need to rethink their career choice. It isn't like this is LA or Chicago."

"Maybe," Timothy replied. "But what about the Katie Douglas murder? Or Linda Echols for that matter? Both of those incidents reek of big-city crimes."

"True. However, cases like those are such a rare occurrence around here. Or so I hope…"

"Listen," the chief continued. "The more Chief Garcia and I discussed his mentoring initiative, the more I thought about our department and how vital a program like that could be for us. We've talked a lot about mental health here and the benefits of checking in with one another to make sure we're all in a good headspace. While the higher-ups have provided a variety of resources, I think a mentorship program would be a great addition to the work we're already doing to improve the team's overall well-being."

Chief Mitchell signaled Officer Davis, who began placing white envelopes in front of each officer.

"I've already taken the liberty of assigning mentees to each of the veteran officers. The name of the person you've been teamed with is inside the envelopes that Davis is passing around."

Nia's legs bounced underneath the table as she antici-
pated who she'd be paired with.

"Ouch," she hissed when her knee hit the metal edge.

Once again, Drew's head turned slightly toward her.
That look of irritation had reappeared. This time, Nia
wanted to say, *Stop taking your frustrations out on me!*
But instead she pressed her hand against her knee, attempt-
ing to rub the pain away without making another sound.

As Officer Davis neared their section, Drew's head adamantly shook from side to side. "I highly doubt that the chief
would ask me to mentor someone. Not when I've just been
chosen to head up the biggest investigation of my career."

"That's *exactly* why he would've assigned you to a mentee," Timothy argued. "What better way to learn the ropes
than to watch a pro catch a killer firsthand?"

"Thanks for the reassurance," Drew deadpanned. "But
no thanks to a rookie getting in the way of my work—"

He paused when Officer Davis approached his table.

"Hey, Officer Taylor, congratulations again on landing
that Douglas case."

"Thanks, man. I appreciate you putting in a good word
for me."

"No problem. The accolades were well-earned after the
way you took charge of that crime scene."

Nia held her breath when Officer Davis handed him an
envelope.

"Oh, no," Drew huffed, refusing to take it. "That can't be
for me. I was just telling Tim that Chief Mitchell wouldn't
have assigned a mentee to me. I've already got my hands
full."

Officer Davis flipped the envelope over and eyed the
name on the front. "I don't know what to tell you, other
than the fact that this clearly says 'Officer Drew Taylor.'"

Emitting a low grunt, Drew snatched it from his hand. "Fine. I'll talk to the chief once this meeting is over."

"Suit yourself. But I think you'd be an excellent mentor to one of our rookies."

"I couldn't agree more," Timothy added.

After Officer Davis moved on to another table, Nia noticed Timothy push Drew's envelope toward him.

"Aren't you gonna open it?" he asked. "See who you've been assigned to?"

"Nope. Because it doesn't matter. I can't be a part of the program. And it's not that I don't think this is a great idea. It's fantastic. I just don't have time for it."

Nia wished she were bold enough to interject. To tell Drew how having a rookie by his side to assist in his investigation would be an asset rather than a disruption. An extra set of eyes on case files, surveillance footage and crime scenes would only bring him closer to solving Katie's murder. But rather than intervene, she remained silent for fear of him biting her head off.

"So what are you gonna do if Chief Mitchell insists you take on a mentee?" Timothy asked.

"Quit."

"Yeah, right."

As the officers broke into laughter, Nia muttered, "That is so messed up."

Both men slowly swiveled in their chairs.

"I'm sorry," Drew said. "What did you just say?"

Nia's mouth fell open. She hadn't intended for those words to slip out of her head and through her lips.

"You weren't listening in on our conversation," Drew probed, "were you?"

"No! Of course not. I was… I was just—"

He reached back and tapped his hand against her table. "Calm down, Officer Brooks. I'm only kidding."

When he pulled away, his fingers brushed against hers. The rush of electricity that shot up her arm sent Nia falling against the back of her chair.

Just as Drew threw her a strange look, Chief Mitchell banged his knuckles against the podium.

"All right, everybody, let's quiet down for a second so I can wrap this up. Now that you've all had a chance to find out who you've been assigned, I'd like for you to get to know your mentorship partners better. Go out for coffee or lunch. Take time during your breaks to go on ride-alongs together. Share investigative stories. Mentors, be generous in offering up guidance to your mentees. Find ways to help them get acclimated to the department, the community and the rules of the Juniper PD. Most importantly, work on creating real, lasting bonds. Remember, you are your brothers' and sisters' keeper. Now, before we go, does anybody have any questions?"

Drew raised his hand. "Yes, sir. I do."

"Go ahead, Officer Taylor."

"What about those of us whose workloads are too heavy to take on a mentee at this time? Can we withdraw our names, then jump back in the next time around?"

"There is no such thing as a workload being too heavy. We're all swamped. It's called sacrifice. And you'd be the perfect mentor, Officer Taylor. Especially with this case you're currently working. Three sets of eyes are better than two. Consider yourself lucky to be adding another person to your team of investigators. Now," Chief Mitchell proceeded, looking around the room without giving Drew a chance to respond. "Any other questions?"

"When does the program start?" Timothy asked.

"Immediately. And I expect for the mentors to take the lead. Reach out to your mentees first. You all are the more experienced of the two. So lead by example. Set something up, then get moving on the mentoring." He paused, glancing around once again. "Anything else?"

A quiet murmur swept through the room as officers spoke quietly among themselves.

"Okay, then," Chief Mitchell said, "this meeting is adjourned. As always, my door is open if anyone would like to stop by and talk in private."

Drew pushed away from the table and jumped to his feet. "Yeah, I'll be the first one doing just that."

"Let it go, Taylor," Timothy said. "The chief has spoken, and I don't think he's going to change his mind. Not to mention I think he's right."

"Yeah, well, we'll see about that. He may be singing a different tune once we talk one-on-one about all the pressure I'm under." Drew snatched up his unopened envelope and shoved it inside his back pocket. "I'll let you know how it goes."

Nia watched as he trudged out of the room. She'd been so wrapped up in his and Timothy's conversation that she hadn't noticed Officer Davis slide her envelope onto the table.

She stared at it, praying that she'd been assigned someone who, unlike Drew, would be enthusiastic about the program and happy to mentor her.

Timothy stood as she tore it open. "Who'd you get, Officer Brooks?"

"I don't know. Let's see…"

Her stomach dropped at the sight of the bold black letters typed across the page.

"So?" Timothy said. "Who's the lucky mentor?"

She turned the paper around. He leaned forward. "'Officer Drew Taylor'? Oh, no. And of course you'd be sitting right behind us. I'm sure you overheard our entire conversation."

"I did." Nia shoved the sheet back inside the envelope. "No worries. I'm sure after Officer Taylor has his conversation with the chief, I'll be assigned to someone else."

"Judging by the tone Chief Mitchell took when Drew gave him pushback, that's highly unlikely. But either way, good luck."

"Thanks. I'm definitely gonna need it."

Chapter Three

It'd been almost two weeks since Drew had been assigned as Nia's mentor. And he'd yet to reach out to her. Timothy had been on his case about it, insisting that he set something up before Chief Mitchell stepped in. But Drew wasn't worried. He'd scheduled a reminder to contact her one day this week. For the time being, his mind was focused solely on the Katie Douglas investigation.

The chief had put in a call to the head of the crime lab down in New Vernon to prioritize the evidence collected at the scene and the results were in—neither the blood nor fingerprints matched any offender profiles in CODIS.

Drew was beyond disappointed as he was certain they'd find a pairing. In his mind, Katie's death was too violent an act for the killer not to have any priors. The officer still believed his suspect had murdered before. He just hadn't been caught yet.

The only clue Drew had to go on was the Latimer Park event calendar. He was convinced there was some sort of message behind it. After he and Timothy stopped by the park and picked up a new brochure, they'd pored over every past and upcoming event. They had even spoken with Katie's friends and relatives to find out if she was somehow connected to the park or any of the activities. As far as they knew, she wasn't.

Drew questioned whether there was a husband or boy-friend in the picture. There wasn't. Katie was single, never married and hadn't fallen out with any exes or friends as far as they knew.

The current state of the investigation had left Drew frustrated and stuck back at square one. The case was all he could think about. He didn't want to drop the ball and watch the case go cold, which meant keeping himself completely immersed in it.

But then there was that damn mentoring program, looming in the back of his mind. Drew imagined getting on Chief Mitchell's bad side and losing the case altogether after stalling on contacting Nia.

Just do it, he thought, spewing a string of curses before rolling over to the other side of his king oakwood bed and grabbing his cell phone.

He checked the time. It was almost 6:00 a.m. Nia usually didn't arrive at the station until a little after eight. Drew had no idea why he knew that. Nevertheless, he sent her a text in hopes of finally getting their first meeting over with.

Good morning, Officer Brooks. Officer Taylor here. Are you free for coffee this morning before work? If so, we can meet up at the Cooper's Cake and Coffee on Motley Boulevard near the station at 7:00 a.m. Does that work for you? Let me know.

Drew sent the message, then made his way through the spacious primary bedroom, the soles of his feet cushioned by the warm cork flooring. He lived in the ranch-style home he'd grown up in, which he'd moved into after his parents left for North Carolina a few years back. Once he was convinced that they were in Charlotte to stay, Drew sold the loft that he'd owned across town.

He thought letting go of the place would be tough. He'd owned it since senior year of college and it held a lot of memories—the most recent being one that he'd rather forget.

Stepping inside the white marble bathroom, Drew turned on the shower and grabbed his toothbrush. His mind drifted to the day that his ex-fiancée moved into the loft. Ellody was the one who'd assured him that his bachelor days were over. His home quickly became theirs as she added her own personal touches, leaving an indelible mark on both the decor and the energy.

After their breakup, he knew he couldn't stay there, which was why he'd jumped at the chance to rent out the loft and set up shop in his childhood home. The eventual sale of his place felt cathartic, confirming that he had finally gotten over his ex.

Drew's pinging cell phone pulled his eyes toward the screen. It was a response from Nia.

Good morning, Officer Taylor. Nice to hear from you. Yes, I'm available to meet. I'll see you at Cooper's at 7. Looking forward to it.

Despite the irritation rumbling through his chest, he replied, Great, see you then.

"You're getting thirty minutes, tops," Drew said to himself before composing a message to Timothy.

Hey, meeting up with Brooks for coffee at 7. Let's connect at Latimer Park afterwards. I wanna take a look around the place. See if we can figure something out on the Douglas case. Does 7:45 work for you?

He hit Send, then jumped in the shower. Anxious to get to the park, he decided to give Nia twenty minutes instead.

DREW ENTERED COOPER'S a few minutes late and glanced around for Nia. The 1950s-style café was packed. He moaned at the sight of the line that was practically out the door. Every shiny red table and booth was occupied. Drew had passed on brewing a pot of coffee at home since he'd expected to grab a cup here. But from the looks of the crowd waiting to place their orders, he'd have to get through the meetup without it.

"Officer Taylor!" someone called out from the back of the shop.

Through the throng of patrons, he spotted Nia waving her hand in the air. He acknowledged her with a nod, then made his way across the black-and-white tiled floor toward her table.

As he got closer, Drew noticed how nice she looked. Nia normally wore her hair pulled back into a bun. Today it was down, with soft curls cascading around her slender face. Red lipstick set off her bright, sexy smile. And she wasn't in uniform. Instead, she was wearing a fitted cream cashmere sweater and tight gray jeans.

"Good morning, Officer Taylor," she said, extending her hand. "Thank you again for meeting with me. I've been looking forward to this since…well, since Chief Mitchell assigned you as my mentor."

"Yeah, sorry for the delay in reaching out," he uttered, taking her hand in his. "As you know, I've been working the Katie Douglas case. Things have been tough, considering it's not going as I'd hoped."

"Hmm, I'm sorry to hear that…"

Several seconds passed before Drew realized he was still

holding on to Nia. For some strange reason, he couldn't get past the soft sensation of her palm pressed against his.

Gesturing for Drew to have a seat, Nia asked, "What's going on with the investigation?"

As they settled into the booth, something about her warm tone and concerned expression lowered his guard. "Well, we got the results back from the crime lab, and nothing matched up with a criminal profile in the database…" Drew's voice trailed off when a server placed two drinks and a tray filled with food onto the table. "Wait, what's all this?"

Nia's lips spread into that alluring smile she'd greeted him with. "I got here about fifteen minutes early and noticed it was getting pretty crowded. So I decided I'd better hurry up and order something for us. That way we wouldn't have to wait." She slid a cup and two items wrapped in plastic in front of him. "I didn't know if you'd be hungry. So I ordered a spinach omelet wrap for you. And of course I had to get us both slices of Cooper's famous cinnamon swirl crunch cake."

"Wow. And here I was thinking I'd have to pass on my morning dose of caffeine. Thank you. For all of this." Pulling the lid off the cup, Drew took a sip. "Hold on. How did you know my coffee order? You must've texted Tim and asked him."

"Nope. I've heard you around the station mentioning how you can't get your day started without a cup of dark roast with a splash of soy milk and one packet of raw sugar."

"Hmph, I didn't realize you were paying that much attention to me."

"I—well, I guess I just have good ears, or…" Nia hesitated, wringing her perfectly manicured hands.

"I'm kidding," Drew said, chuckling at how easy it was to throw off the rookie. "Don't worry. I know you're not stalking me or eavesdropping. Even though you *did* jump into my conversation with Tim during that mentorship meeting."

Her tense expression broke into a slight smirk.

"So is this how it's gonna be?" Nia asked. "Are you going to haze me throughout our entire mentorship?"

"I might…" Drew quipped, relaxing against the padded seat cushion. "No, but seriously. I appreciate this. I'm gonna have to take it to go though. I'm meeting Tim at Latimer Park and need to leave soon."

"Oh…okay."

The disappointment in Nia's soft tone was apparent. But her wide eyes appeared hopeful, as if she was waiting for an invitation to ride along with them. Drew wasn't totally against the idea but decided to hold off on extending an invitation.

"What time are you and Officer Braxton meeting up?" she asked.

"About seven forty-five." Drew pulled his cell from his black leather jacket. "Speaking of Tim, he never did confirm. That's not like him."

"Maybe he's sleeping in late?"

"I doubt it. He usually hits the gym every morning at five, and it's almost seven-fifteen. I'm sure he'll get back to me soon. Anyway, why don't we talk a little bit about your past experience and what made you want to become a police officer?"

Nia's brows lifted as she slid to the edge of her seat. The glimmer in her eyes reminded Drew of the excitement he'd felt during his time as a rookie.

"Well," she began, "as you know, I worked as a 9-1-1 operator for eight years before joining the force."

"Right. I did know that."

"There was something about those calls I'd receive and the rush of adrenaline pumping through my body whenever I'd send emergency services out to assist the victims. It made me feel vulnerable and helpless in a strange way. Like there was more I could be doing. Eventually the desire to serve a bigger purpose hit, and I began contemplating making a move to the force."

"Really? Why is that? Our 9-1-1 operators are vital. They're the first point of contact between the victims and law enforcement. Without them, we'd be completely uninformed and disorganized."

"I agree. But for me, I felt the need to be more present. Out there on the front lines, assisting firsthand rather than sitting inside the call center."

"Okay. I feel you on that…"

Drew's voice trailed off when a deep frown overtook Nia's cheery expression.

"There's, um," she began, her tone almost a whisper. "There was one call in particular that really turned things around for me."

"Oh? Which call was that?"

"Linda Echols."

Nia's response disarmed Drew's cool disposition. Recoiling at the pull in his chest, he nodded stiffly. "Yeah… That was a tough one. Were you the operator who handled it?"

"I was. I'll never forget how powerless I felt on the other end of that call, struggling to keep Linda calm while trying to send help. But the responding officers had trouble getting to her house. The attacker got to her before they could. I can still remember the shrill intonations in her screams, and how she kept saying that if he makes his way inside, he's going to kill her." Nia paused, clawing at the napkin underneath her coffee cup. "I was devastated when I heard she'd been found inside her bedroom closet with her throat slashed."

"I hope you're not blaming yourself for any of that."

"I try not to. But I did. For a long time. That guilt is what prompted me to join the force."

"Well I know for a fact that Chief Mitchell was thrilled to welcome you to the department. I mean, he *really* sang your praises in particular. Every chance he'd get, he would talk about how you're an excellent addition to the squad."

"Yeah, that was really nice of him," Nia murmured, her lush lips curling into a half grin.

The sight of her spirits lifting motivated Drew to continue. "I don't know if you're aware of this, but we'd hear little tidbits about which recruits were doing well and standing out. Your name was always at the top of everyone's list. Your sharp instincts, high level of intelligence, dedication to the Juniper community…nothing but good things were spoken about you. So remember that whenever those feelings of guilt start to hit. Let those traits be a reminder that what happened to Linda was in no way your fault. You did all that you could to try and save her. And hey, you never know. Now that you're on the force, maybe you'll get an opportunity to help solve her cold case."

Sitting up a little straighter, Nia's eyes connected with his gaze. "You know what? You're absolutely right."

A loud rumble floated through the air. Drew grabbed his stomach and glanced around the café, hoping no one else heard it. When a soft giggle slipped through Nia's lips, he realized she had.

"Why don't you take at least one bite of that wrap?" she suggested. "Because clearly you're hungry."

He peered down at his phone again. Still no word from Timothy. "Might as well." After noticing she hadn't unwrapped hers, Drew asked, "Aren't you going to eat?"

"I will. Once I get to the station."

"Why don't you eat now? Tim hasn't gotten back to me yet, so I've got time."

Wrinkling her nose, Nia tapped her fingers against the table.

"What's wrong?"

"Nothing. It's just…a little embarrassing."

"What's embarrassing?"

"I'm too nervous to eat," Nia murmured through tight lips.

"Nervous? Why?"

"Is that a real question? I don't think you realize how intimidating you can be, Officer Taylor."

He dropped his wrap and searched her face for a sign of humor. There wasn't one. "I had no idea anyone thought of me as intimidating. Would it help if you start calling me Drew instead of Officer Taylor?"

"It might…" she replied while slowly peeling the plastic off her wrap.

"Good. So tell me, Officer Brooks. When it comes to this mentorship program, what are you expecting from me?"

"Now hold on. It wouldn't be fair for me to call you Drew if you don't call me Nia, would it?"

"I guess it wouldn't be, *Nia*. So go on. I'm listening."

"Well, aside from all the things Chief Mitchell mentioned during the meeting, I'd love to just shadow you. If that wouldn't be too much trouble…"

"It wouldn't be. And before you continue, can I just apologize for whatever you overheard me saying to Tim at that meeting? I'd just been assigned the Douglas investigation, and—"

"You don't have to explain anything. I get it. I figured I'd find a way to win you over eventually. Hopefully the coffee and breakfast was a good start."

"Oh, this was an excellent start. By the way, how much do I owe you?" he asked, reaching for his wallet.

"You don't owe me a thing. Consider this a thank-you for taking the time to meet with me."

A streak of guilt stabbed Drew in the gut. He'd been so resistant to meeting with Nia, and she had turned out to be more gracious than he ever could've imagined. "You're welcome. Next time is on me. Now, back to you wanting to shadow me."

"Yes. I'd love to help out with the Katie Douglas case however I can. Of course I wouldn't get in the way of things or overstep my bounds. But it would be great if I could experience the ins and outs of a murder investigation firsthand."

"I don't think that would be a problem. But let me talk to Tim first. He's my partner, and out of respect for him, I should figure out what role he's going to play beforehand. Is that cool?"

"Of course. And just know that I'm willing to take on whatever role I can, no matter how big or small."

"I'll keep that in mind…" After checking the time on his cell again, Drew scrolled through his notifications. Nothing from Timothy. "We should probably head out. I still wanna take a look around Latimer Park before I check in at the station."

Nia was slow to gather her things. Judging by her fallen expression, Drew sensed she didn't want to leave.

"Thanks again for inviting me to coffee," she said. "This was good. I think it may have been the most we've ever spoken since I started working for the Juniper PD."

"Oh, now you're trying to make me out to be some stand-offish introvert," he joked, following her toward the exit.

"That could not be further from what I'm saying!"

As he held open the door, Drew couldn't help but notice the sway in Nia's curvy hips. She brushed up against him, her touch sending an electric shot straight to his groin.

Don't even go there...

When they reached Nia's silver Acura, she clicked the alarm. "I'll see you back at the station. Good luck at Latimer Park. I hope you and Officer Braxton find something useful."

"Yeah, about that. I still haven't heard from Tim. And as Chief Mitchell likes to say, two sets of eyes are better than one. So, if you want, you can follow me to the park."

Pressing her hands together, Nia replied, "I'd like that," before the words were hardly out of his mouth. "I've got my evidence collection kit in the trunk, too. So if I stumble upon anything viable, I'll be prepared to collect it."

Drew couldn't help but chuckle at her enthusiasm. It was actually endearing.

You're doing it again, he thought before backing away.

"Sounds good," he told her. "I'll lead the way."

"Hey!" Nia called out just as he reached his car. "I forgot to mention that I know Latimer Park's recreation manager. If she's there, I'll see if we can get in and talk to her about that event calendar you found on the victim. Maybe she knows something."

"That would be awesome. Thanks."

Drew climbed inside his car and glanced in the rearview mirror, making sure Nia was behind him before pulling out. When she waved, he gave her a thumbs-up, then left the lot. As he drove down Sandpiper Road, wise words from his father popped into his head.

The universe works in mysterious ways...

Considering Nia's unexpected involvement in the investigation, Drew thought of how interesting it would be if she became the catalyst to solving the case.

Chapter Four

Nia eased up on the accelerator, realizing she'd been tailing Drew's car way too closely. But she couldn't help herself. The thrill of working the Douglas case had her emotions coursing full speed. Determination surged the strongest as she was eager to prove her capabilities, and hopefully, solidify her spot in the investigation.

Drew's cool, laid-back attitude had come as a pleasant surprise. Nia assumed it would take weeks, if not longer, to crack his hardened demeanor. But their meetup, albeit brief, gave her hope that his mentorship wouldn't be nearly as dreadful as she'd expected.

The get-together did nothing, however, to quell Nia's feelings for him. If anything, they'd intensified. Oddly enough, she didn't feel as though the sparks were one-sided. There were several moments when Drew appeared a bit flirty. The way he'd wink at her after saying something funny or flash a suggestive half smile while agreeing with a point she'd made. Those small gestures hadn't sent warm sensations stirring through her center for nothing.

Hold on, Nia told herself mid-thought. *Don't go getting ahead of yourself...*

Drew's bright taillights pulled her back into the moment

as they drove across the Sparrow Lane Bridge. Nia's heartbeat quickened when Latimer Park appeared in the distance.

Cottonwood and Early Richmond cherry trees were scattered along the outskirts of the lush, sloped landscape. Stay-at-home parents bordered the playground as children rode the merry-go-round and climbed monkey bars. Tennis lessons were in session, and several young men were practicing their free throws on the basketball court.

It was hard to believe that such a beautiful, active space was now tainted by a possible connection to Katie Douglas's murder.

Just when Drew made a slight turn onto Candlewood Avenue, he reached out the window and signaled to Nia, then quickly pulled over. She parked behind him, craning her neck to see what was going on.

After waiting for him to get out of the car, Nia peered through his rear windshield and saw Drew's cell phone glued to his ear. A few minutes later her phone rang. It was him.

"Hey, what's going on?" she asked.

"Chief Mitchell just called. We need to get back to the station. Something's happened to Tim."

"*What?* Is he okay?"

"I don't know. But judging by the chief's tone, it sounds serious. He just got a call from Tim's mother saying that he's been rushed to the emergency room. Hopefully Chief will know more by the time we get there."

"Got it. I'm right behind you."

NIA AND DREW pulled into the station's parking lot and charged into the building. While he headed straight for Chief Mitchell's office, she stopped at her desk.

"Keep me posted!" she told him.

He spun around, his brows wrinkled with confusion. "Wait, you're not coming with me?"

"I—I didn't know if you wanted me there."

"I definitely want you there. Whatever's going on, I could use all the support I can get."

The officer's worried expression almost prompted Nia to wrap him in a warm embrace. Instead she nodded, following him to the chief's office.

They barely reached the doorway before Drew asked, "What's going on with Tim? Any updates since we last spoke?"

Chief Mitchell ran his hands through his thinning gray hair. "Have a seat, you two."

While Nia sat directly across from the chief, Drew paced the creaking wood floor.

"Chief, you're scaring me," he said. "What happened to Tim?"

"He, uh…he was in a really bad car accident on the way home from the gym this morning. It was a hit-and-run. According to a witness, another vehicle that was driving behind him accelerated, then rammed into the back of Tim's car. He spun out of control and slammed into a tree."

"Oh my God," Drew moaned, slumping into the chair next to Nia's.

"He was thrown from the vehicle and suffered several injuries," Chief Mitchell continued. "A concussion, broken bones, a punctured lung…"

"Is he showing any signs of brain damage?" Nia asked.

"They're not sure yet. The doctors are still running tests. But the good news is Tim's breathing on his own. He's been put in a medically induced coma just in case he experienced any brain swelling and to give his body a chance to heal."

"Was the witness able to get a license plate number?" Drew croaked.

"No, unfortunately. But he did say that the collision seemed intentional. Instead of going after the driver, he went to help Tim and call an ambulance."

"I should probably go to the hospital," Drew said. "Check on his family and make sure they're doing okay."

The chief nodded in agreement. "Good idea. I'm sure his mother would appreciate that. And I hate to bring this up, but now that Tim is out of commission, what are we going to do about the Katie Douglas investigation?"

"Yeah," Drew uttered, running his hand along the back of his neck. "I can't head that up alone. I'm gonna need a partner."

"Do you have anyone in mind?"

The question straightened Nia's back. Her head swiveled from Chief Mitchell to Drew, then back to the chief.

"I do, actually," Drew responded. "Officer Davis was the first person I thought of since he and I worked so well together at the crime scene."

The chief's gaze drifted toward Nia. She bit down on her jaw, desperate to throw her hat in the ring. But she held back. She'd been on the force less than a year. Officer Davis had way more experience. Nia knew she didn't stand a chance against him.

"What about Officer Brooks?" Chief Mitchell asked.

Huh?

She perked up, her face growing hot with anticipation while awaiting Drew's response.

"I'm sorry," he muttered. "Come again?"

"I said, what about Officer Brooks?"

As Drew remained silent, Nia held a hand in the air. "Should, um…should I leave, or—"

"No, no," the chief said. "You should stay. Maybe help plead your case on why you'd make a good partner on this investigation."

She turned to Drew, cringing at the slight scowl on his face.

"That won't be necessary," Drew huffed. "Because it's not gonna happen. Now I agreed to the whole mentoring thing. But this is where I draw the line. I need a veteran officer by my side who's familiar with crime scenes and evidence analysis. Someone who can put leads and tips and pieces of the investigative puzzle together to get this case solved."

Chief Mitchell kept silent while sipping from his World's Best Granddad mug. His lack of a response seemed to set Drew off as the officer sprang from his chair, continuing his rant while pacing the floor once more.

Holding her hand to her chest, Nia pulled in a sharp breath of air and peered over at Drew. The intensity in his wild eyes and erratic hand gestures were jarring. He was speaking about her as if she weren't even in the room. His behavior was far from that of the cool guy he'd appeared to be at Cooper's—the one who seemingly welcomed her into the investigation. Now that things had gotten real, the chief's suggestion sent him spiraling.

"Please, Officer Taylor," Chief Mitchell said. "Calm down. Have a seat. Let's talk this out. Do you need some water, or coffee—"

"No," Drew interrupted, throwing himself into the chair. "I'm fine. I'm just worried about Tim. And the investigation, of course."

"Which is all perfectly understandable. Do you still think you're capable of handling the case considering the news about Tim? Because if you're not, I can always pass it on to another officer."

"Of course I am, Chief. Regardless of what's going on around me, I'm completely up for it."

Tension sucked the air from the room. Nia clenched her toes inside her combat boots while awaiting Chief Mitchell's response. But he just sat there, patting his fist against the desk. Judging by the look on Drew's poker face, he was done pleading his case.

Finally, after several moments of pained silence, the chief said, "Officer Taylor, keep in mind that Officer Brooks isn't new to the Juniper PD. She's worked within the department for years."

"Yeah, as a 9-1-1 op—"

"Hold on. I'm well aware of her former position. My point is, Officer Brooks is familiar with this town, the rules of the department and the inner workings of crime and apprehension. She won Telecommunicator of the Year five years in a row. That award isn't easy to come by."

Chief Mitchell paused, as if waiting for Drew to reply. But the officer remained silent.

"What I'm saying is, Officer Brooks is special. She's sharp. Her attention to detail is uncanny. Her communication and leadership skills are exceptional. The level of care and respect she's shown to victims is unmatched. She has helped solved crimes by simply asking the right questions during 9-1-1 calls. You don't come by those traits easily or often. When you do, you have to utilize them. What better way to do that than to partner with Officer Brooks on this case?"

"With all those accolades," Drew grumbled, "maybe you should just assign the case to her."

"Keep it up and I just might."

That's it, Nia thought, no longer able to withstand the awkward conversation. Just as she grasped the arms of her chair to stand, Drew emitted an exasperated sigh.

"Fine. I'll partner with Ni—I mean Officer Brooks. Not that I have a choice in the matter," he added under his breath.

"Good decision," Chief Mitchell said, ignoring the second half of Drew's response. "Officer Brooks, are you good with this?"

"I am, thank you. I really appreciate your kind words as well as this opportunity."

"Of course you do," Drew whispered toward his feet.

Nia glared in his direction, that crush she'd had on him fading by the minute.

"It's all well-earned," the chief told her. "Now, I'll be expecting a report from you two on the Douglas case in the next few days. Officer Taylor, maybe you can take Brooks down to Shelby's Candy Factory so she can assess the crime scene in person. Who knows—maybe she'll come across something that you and the other officers missed."

It was obvious that the chief was baiting Drew. Nia braced herself, waiting to see if he'd bite.

"I'd love for that to happen," he responded, holding his arms out at his sides. "If she does, that just means we'll be one step closer to solving the case."

"Now *that's* what I like to hear," Chief Mitchell boomed. "Teamwork. It makes the dream work, right?"

"Oh, please…" Drew hissed through clenched teeth.

"All right, you two," the chief continued. "Unless you've got something else for me, I think we're done."

Charging to the door, Drew said, "I'm going to the hospital to check on Tim. I'll have my phone if anyone needs me."

"Hey!" Chief Mitchell called out. "Be sure to check in with me as soon as you can. Let me know how he's doing."

"Will do."

Drew left the office without giving Nia so much as a glance. Ignoring the uncertainty banging against her temples, she slowly stood.

"Thank you again, Chief. I promise I won't let you down."

"I know you won't. That's why I assigned this case to you. Now get out there and prove Officer Taylor and anybody else who may be doubting you wrong."

"Yes, sir."

Those words were all it took to send Nia back to her cubicle with her head held high. Just as she sat down, someone approached from behind. It was Drew.

"Here you go," he said, slamming a file down on the desk. "This is everything I've got on the Douglas case. I would advise you to read through every single word of it and examine those crime scene photos from top to bottom. We'll make plans to go to the candy factory in the next day or so. For now, I just need to make sure Tim is okay."

"Understood. Please send Tim my well wishes. And hey, Drew? Just so you know, I'm really looking forward to working on this investigation with you. I may not be the most experienced officer on the force, but I promise I'll do everything I can to help solve this case."

He responded with a grunt before walking away.

"Nice chat," Nia mumbled.

Shrugging it off, she reminded herself that getting justice for Katie was all that mattered, whether Drew wanted her help or not.

Chapter Five

Drew felt like crap as he pulled back into the station. Seeing Tim connected to all those tubes while surrounded by machines, concerned doctors and worried loved ones had been devastating. It was a reminder that anything could happen at any given moment. And there were bigger concerns in life than him being partnered with a rookie cop.

The hospital visit was a wake-up call that left him feeling ashamed of his meltdown. The disrespect he'd shown toward Chief Mitchell and Nia was unacceptable, making his first order of business a talk with his boss, then his newly appointed partner.

Drew entered the department and made a beeline for the chief's office. The door was open. He approached it cautiously, knocking lightly on the frame.

"Hey, Chief, you got a sec?"

"I do," he replied, without looking up from his cell phone. "But hang on. Chief Garcia from Finchport is gonna be calling me any minute now. He wants an update on how our mentorship program is working out. Speaking of which…" He paused, finally peering up at Drew. "How's the mentoring going between you and Officer Brooks? Last I heard you two hadn't connected yet."

"Actually we did connect. Over coffee this morning."

The chief set his phone to the side. "Well, that wasn't what I expected to hear. But it certainly makes me happy. Is it safe to assume you two got along okay?"

"Yes. We got along just fine."

"Good. Because after the way things went during that meeting earlier..." Chief Mitchell hesitated, then pointed at Drew. "You're one of our main leaders around here, Officer Taylor. And I expect for you to act like it. At all times. The behavior you displayed in my office earlier today in front of Officer Brooks was disgraceful. You're better than that. So I'm hoping to never see that side of you again."

"That's actually why I stopped by, sir. I wanted to apologize. You're right. And you have my word that it'll never happen again."

"Apology accepted. Was I your first stop since returning to the office?"

"Yes, you were."

"I'm guessing you know what the second stop needs to be?"

Drew shoved his hands inside his pockets and walked back toward the doorway. "Yes, sir, I do."

"Good. Trust me, Officer Brooks is gonna be a great asset to your investigation. Now get to work. Oh, and thanks for the update on Tim. I'm glad to hear the doctors are planning to reduce the meds that are keeping him in the coma. Did they say what they're expecting to happen once the dosage is lowered?"

"They're hoping he'll open his eyes. Respond to sights and sounds. Grip his mother's hand. Things like that."

The conversation was interrupted when Chief Mitchell's phone rang. "That's Chief Garcia. We'll catch up later. In the meantime, you know what you've gotta do."

"I do. And I'm on my way to do it now."

Drew sauntered toward the rookie cubicle area. Heads turned as he appeared to be talking to himself. But he was practicing which version of an apology he would give to Nia.

When he approached the desk, her chair was empty.

Good, he thought, realizing he wasn't quite ready for a face-to-face just yet. The day had already been heavy enough. Plus he couldn't seem to mentally compose a decent enough apology.

"Hey, Officer Taylor," a soft voice murmured behind him. "Were you looking for me?"

Dammit...

"Yuh—yeah," he stammered. Noticing she'd gone back to the formalities, he contemplated reminding her that she could call him Drew. But he resisted. After the way he'd behaved earlier, he didn't blame her for shutting down their friendly rapport. "Do you have a minute?"

Nia set a freshly poured cup of coffee on her desk and sat down, pointing to a chair in the corner. "I do. Please, have a seat. How is Officer Braxton doing?"

"He's already showing some slight signs of improvement. I was just telling Chief Mitchell that the doctors are hoping to start pulling him out of the coma tomorrow."

"Oh, good. I've been putting in my fair share of prayers all morning." She went quiet, her dazzling deep brown eyes searching Drew's face. "How are you holding up?"

I don't deserve your kindness, he almost blurted. The amount of concern this woman was showing toward him was inexplicable.

"I'm holding up okay. Knowing that Tim is getting better has me feeling cautiously hopeful. Thanks for asking."

Drew rocked back in his chair, suddenly lost for words. The fragmented apologies he'd just mentally rehearsed completely slipped from his mind now that he was in Nia's presence.

Freestyle something, he told himself, glancing over at her. She stared back expectantly, making no attempt to fill in the awkward gap of silence. He didn't blame her. This situation was on him to fix.

"Nia, if it's okay that I still call you that, I need to address the way I behaved this morning during our meeting with Chief Mitchell. I don't wanna use Tim's accident as an excuse, but hearing that he'd been hurt sent my mind reeling. Then after finding out how bad off he was, I honestly didn't think he was going to make—"

His voice broke underneath the weight of his words. When Nia reached out and clutched his hand, warmth radiated from her smooth skin, easing his pain like a soothing balm. "Look, I'm getting off track here. I want to apologize for the way I treated you. You didn't deserve that. And just to be clear, I have no doubt that you'll be an asset to this investigation."

"Thank you, Drew. I appreciate you saying that. Apology accepted." She held his gaze, flashing that same bright smile that had caught his attention when he'd entered Cooper's. "Listen, why don't we forget about what happened earlier and start over with a clean slate?"

"I'd like that."

"Good." She opened the case file and flipped through the police report. "Now that we've gotten all that out of the way, come closer. I'll go over what I've been working on since you've been gone."

"Oh? So you've been working my case without me?" he teased in an attempt to lighten the mood.

"I've been working *our* case without you. But anyway, I was looking through these notes and saw that Katie Douglas's family found her cell phone inside her apartment, which they turned over to law enforcement."

"Right. Officer Mills is downloading and researching all the data now. Once he's done, he's gonna provide me, well, now *us*, with all the pertinent info. So we'll find out who she'd been calling, texting, messaging on social media… those sorts of things."

"Yes, I spoke with Officer Mills about that. He confirmed that he'll be tracking her digital footprint as well, which is good. I'm curious to know where she'd been prior to her murder. In the meantime, I asked if I could take a look at the apps on her phone. One that stood out was the Someone for Everyone dating app. Did you know she was a member?"

"No, I didn't. But after speaking with her family, I did find out that she wasn't seeing anybody."

"As far as they knew."

Hunching his broad shoulders, Drew leaned in and studied the notes. "That's true. I just assumed they would know. Especially her sister. They seemed pretty close."

"Trust me, that doesn't mean a thing. Take my younger sister Ivy, for example. I used to think we were as tight as could be. Then one day I found out she'd been dating some guy for an entire year who I knew nothing about. People oftentimes hide things from those they're closest to. Especially when it comes to relationships."

"You make a good point. With that being said, we should reach out to the app's administrator as soon as possible."

"I'm already on it," Nia responded before flipping open her notebook. "I reached out to their customer service department requesting access to Katie's account. We need to know who she'd been in contact with and whether she made plans to meet up with anyone before her murder. Since so many people communicate solely through the app, there may be information we won't find in her emails, text messages and call log."

"Wow. You really are on it. I love the way you're taking such strong initiative." Drew hesitated, fiddling with the crown on his stainless steel watch. "Wait, you seem to know an awful lot about this whole dating app thing."

Nia ignored the remark. But her subtle smirk let him know she'd heard him loud and clear. "So anyway, I'm still waiting to hear back from the company. I had to contact them through the app since I couldn't find a phone number. I'll let you know as soon as they reach out."

"Sounds good. Nice work on all this—"

"Oh, wait!" she interrupted. "Before I forget, I got ahold of Latimer Park's recreation manager. Her name is Dawn Frazier by the way. She said that Katie's name doesn't ring a bell. After searching through the activity database, she found that Katie had never registered for any classes or programs. So as far as Dawn knows, she was in no way connected to the park. But Dawn did say we could come by anytime to speak with her and search the premises."

Drew eyed Nia while fidgeting with his goatee. He would've expected the average rookie to passively wait for him to return from the hospital, set up a meeting, then sit down together to discuss the next moves. But not Nia. Clearly she was well above average, proving every word that Chief Mitchell had spoken about her to be true.

Two traits he'd failed to mention, however, were her tenacity and assertiveness—characteristics Drew found to be most attractive in a woman.

"Again," he said, "good work. Thank you."

"No problem. I was thinking—maybe you should send a patrol car out to Latimer Park to keep an eye on things.

You know, just in case the killer left that event calendar at the crime scene to hint at what might be coming next."

"That's not a bad idea. Even if Katie isn't directly linked, there could still be some sort of connection. We'll run it by Chief Mitchell and see what he thinks. If he gives us the okay, I'll get someone assigned to the job as soon as possible."

"Excellent."

Drew reached for one of the crime scene photos just as Nia closed the file. Their hands met. His fingers slid between hers, rousing a heat so intense that he lurched in his chair.

"Sorry," he uttered, slow to pull away.

Nia's narrowing eyes drifted from his hand to his lips. "So…what's next?"

"Why don't we head to the candy factory so you can check out the crime scene. Then we'll stop by Latimer Park if there's still enough daylight."

Rolling away from the desk, she grabbed her tote. "Sounds like a plan."

"Cool. I'll get my stuff and meet you out front."

While Nia headed toward the lobby, Drew watched her walk away, his pupils shifting to the swing of her graceful stride.

Turn around, he thought, tearing himself away from the hypnotic sight.

The officer couldn't decide which was more impressive—Nia's beauty or her savvy. Either way, he was glad to have her on his team.

Chapter Six

Nia stretched out on her cream leather sofa, kneading her fist into her quads after an intense spin class. The day had been long. She'd stayed at the station way past six, then stopped by the grocery store before heading to the gym.

Cozying up against a green suede pillow, Nia was hit with a bout of loneliness. The chilly autumn night left her wishing she had someone to come home to. It'd been almost two years since she had been in a serious relationship. In the past week, she and Drew had spent countless hours together, which only magnified her single status. It almost felt like punishment, working so closely with the man she'd been pining after for years.

Landing a case of this magnitude early in her rookie career was a dream. Nia had hoped that fact alone would hold her attention so that she wouldn't be laser-focused on Drew. Yet the complete opposite had occurred. Seeing him in uniform, taking charge and handling the investigation with such skill and ease, only made him more appealing.

Once the pair had teamed up, Nia realized she'd only scratched the surface of who really Drew was. Underneath the tough exterior was a thoughtful man who always took her thoughts and theories into consideration. That had been pretty surprising after the meltdown he'd had in Chief

Mitchell's office. But aside from his investigative acumen and meticulous critical thinking skills, it was Drew's appreciation of her contributions that impressed Nia the most.

The drawback, however, was that her feelings for Drew were growing beyond her control. Her slight crush had been manageable. But these new emotions were beginning to get the best of her. And it was frustrating that she couldn't do anything about it.

Nia closed her eyes. Mulled over the moments alone she and Drew had been spending together. Just that afternoon when they were inside the cluttered evidence room he'd slipped past her, his hard chest pressing against her back. She'd gasped and spun around, her breasts brushing against his taut bicep as he reached out to steady her.

Self-control left her body when she quivered within his grip. Drew just stood there, his parted lips indicating he'd felt her reaction. Those massive hands lingered on her hips. Their mouths were so close that as he exhaled, she inhaled the sweet scent of cinnamon espresso on his breath.

Nia's desire for Drew no longer appeared one-sided. But dating a colleague was still off-limits. Being a Juniper police officer meant everything to her. If she and Drew got together, then broke up, her dream job would become a nightmare as Nia knew she didn't have the stomach to face an ex every day.

"Oh, well," she sighed, turning up the volume on the Tennis Channel. As Chanda Rubin reviewed the day's top matches, she grabbed her phone and swiped open the Someone for Everyone app. There were several messages, but none from the administrator in response to her Katie Douglas request.

Drew had been right about one thing—Nia did know

her way around the dating app. What he didn't know was that she'd been a member for almost a year.

After Linda Echols's murder, Nia had grown depressed. She became obsessed with work and began isolating herself socially. Friends insisted that she needed to get out more and start dating, if for nothing else than to help take her mind off the tragic death. It had taken quite a bit of convincing on their part. But after they assured Nia she could easily connect with the perfect match through a dating app as opposed to a bar or club, she gave in and joined Someone for Everyone.

Nia had only been out with a few of the members. Two of them lived in nearby towns and one resided in Denver. None had worked out. But she hadn't given up hope just yet.

After swiping through several lackluster profiles, Nia clicked on her inbox and scrolled through the messages. She stopped at the sight of a man's profile picture. He appeared tall, his slim-fitting navy suit tailored to a tee. His flawless deep brown skin glowed as he flashed a sexy, mischievous half smile. His dark, piercing eyes looked as though they were staring right at her. The gaze was somewhat haunting, but at the same time intoxicating.

"Hmm…" Nia murmured before opening his message.

Hello, beautiful. My name is Shane Anderson, and I am new to the Juniper area. I just stumbled across your profile, and I must say, you are quite lovely. I would love to get to know you better. If the feeling is mutual, please feel free to respond to this message. I hope to hear from you soon…xx, Shane

Nia reread the message at least three times. It may have been short, but it was one of the more gentlemanly introductions that she'd received. Most men asked what her plans were for the evening and whether she was available to hook up. And by *hook up*, it was clear they weren't referring to dinner or drinks.

Curiosity coursed through Nia's fingers as she clicked on his profile. The headline read, Shane, 38. Always up for meeting great people and experiencing new adventures. About Me: Works hard as a wealth management advisor Monday through Friday so that I can venture out and explore the world on weekends. Loves to laugh. Hates Brussels sprouts. Might challenge you to a dance-off in the middle of the club.

A soft smile teased Nia's lips as she took a sip of Merlot. "So you're handsome, smart and seem to have a good sense of humor. Nice start."

She scrolled down and continued reading.

What I'm Looking For: A woman who isn't afraid to laugh at herself, loves to travel, doesn't mind dog cuddles, is confident and secure, and knows what she wants. If we're a match, she would totally be down to explore this thing called life with me.

"I think this one might have potential," she said before opening his photo album. There was a picture of him sitting out on a massive backyard deck, a golden retriever nearby. Then one of him rock climbing inside the Pier 48 Fitness entertainment complex. From the look of his cut physique, he spent a fair amount of time in the gym.

The rest of the album contained an array of travel photos—from deep-sea fishing in Cabo San Lucas to skydiving along the Amalfi Coast. As his profile headline stated, Shane did indeed seem to live an adventurous life. Nia wondered if she could keep up. Aside from becoming a police officer, the most daring thing she'd ever done was take a midnight ghost tour through downtown Colorado Springs one Halloween weekend.

Deciding that Shane had potential, Nia replied to his message.

Hello, Shane. Thank you for your message. It's nice to "e-meet" you. My name is Nia, and as a lifelong resident of Juniper, I do hope you're enjoying my hometown thus far. To answer your question, yes, I would like to get to know you better. I'll start things off. After viewing your profile, I saw that you are quite daring. Have you found any fun activities here in town that have satisfied your adventure-seeking spirit? If not, I've got a few ideas. Looking forward to hearing from you...xx, Nia

"Now I just need to google thrilling things to do in Juniper."

Soon after she hit Send, Nia's phone pinged.

"That was quick."

A mix of hope and excitement simmered in her chest as Nia reopened the text thread between her and Shane. There were no new messages.

"What, what's happening here?"

She refreshed the page. Still nothing new.

Then an email notification appeared at the top of the screen. The message was from Drew, and the subject read "Case Report for Chief Mitchell—Final."

Nia's mind immediately shifted to thoughts of the investigation. The pair had spent the majority of the day composing the report. It had gotten late, and Drew knew she didn't want to miss her spin class. So he was kind enough to let her go while he stayed back and added the final touches.

Hey Nia, the message read. I hope your class went well. I've attached the final case report for the chief. Take a look and let me know what you think. If you don't have any changes, we'll send it first thing in the morning. Looking forward to hearing from you. Have a good night. Drew

Nia clicked on the attachment and scanned the report. They'd started off by bringing Chief Mitchell up to speed on their visit to Shelby's Candy Factory. For over two hours, the officers combed the area where Katie's body had been discovered. Just when they were about to give up, Nia found a piece of cardboard underneath the cold pressing unit. It contained a dirty shoeprint impression that looked to be the sole of a size eleven in men's. Luckily for them, the distinct treads with beveled edges and slanting lugs were clearly visible. Drew took photos and sent the fiberboard off to the crime lab for testing.

Through a shoe-sole pattern classification system database, Nia discovered that the print belonged to a Lacrosse AeroHead Sport hunting boot. Despite knowing the print could belong to anyone as there had been plenty of people in and out of the factory, she and Drew were hoping that the print would prove viable in helping to track down their killer.

Next was a summary of their visit to Latimer Park. After inspecting the area, nothing appeared suspicious. Dawn, the recreation manager, wasn't able to share much more than she already had during her phone conversation with Nia. Their brief meeting ended with her promising to keep an eye out and let law enforcement know if anything strange occurred.

After getting the okay from Chief Mitchell, Drew had assigned Officer Davis to patrol the park. Days went by with no abnormal activity. Davis questioned whether the crumpled event calendar found at the crime scene was relevant to their case.

"Don't give up," Drew had told him. "You never know what we may find."

But nothing could convince Officer Davis that the Latimer Park stakeout wasn't a waste of time. He didn't think the killer would make a move with a patrol car present. Nia and Drew felt his presence would deter the killer from making a move at all. In the midst of the debate, Davis requested that the stakeout be called off. So Drew wrapped up the report asking that Chief Mitchell make the final decision.

Nia replied to the email confirming the report was good to go, then took another sip of wine. She needed a break. Ever since the chief partnered her with Drew, the case was all she thought about. It was difficult enough knowing there was a killer on the streets of Juniper terrorizing the community. But the pressure to prove herself while struggling to not overstep her bounds had become an even heavier burden to bear. The search for balance was beginning to wear on Nia and a reprieve was in order—which was why the message from Shane had come at the perfect time.

Just as she grabbed the remote and turned to the Oxygen channel, her phone pinged again. This time, it was a text from Drew.

Hey, it's me again. Thanks for the green light on the report. On another note, Officer Davis talked to Chief Mitchell this evening, and Chief decided to stop the surveillance on Latimer Park. I'm really disappointed as I'm sure you are too since we both believe that the event calendar is no coincidence. I'll talk to the boss in the morning and try to change his mind. Fingers crossed. Have a good night.

Dread poured over Nia as she slammed her phone against the couch. Of course the calendar was no coincidence. But trying to defend their hunch without further proof, signs of suspicious activity or a viable connection between Katie and the park seemed impossible.

Nia stared at Drew's message, rereading it a couple more times before composing a response that wouldn't reflect the anger ringing inside her head.

Thanks for the update. I'm really disappointed to hear that as well. Let's just hope that Chief Mitchell is right and nothing comes of the calendar being left at the scene. Hope you have a good night as well.

After sending the message, Nia opened the Quick Eats app and ordered a buffalo chicken sandwich with a side of loaded fries instead of the salad. News of the canceled stakeout left her craving comfort food.

Just as she refilled her wine glass, her cell pinged again. Nia assumed it was Drew and swiped open her phone without checking the notification. The Someone for Everyone heart-shaped icon flashed on the screen, indicating she had a new message.

She sat straight up and opened it. A text from Shane appeared.

Hello Nia. It's nice to "e-meet" you as well. Beautiful name, btw. Thank you for your quick response. Did I mention that I love a woman who's prompt? But anyway, as I'd stated in my previous message, I'm new to town. I recently began working for a brokerage firm, and let's just say I've been earning every single penny! Once my schedule frees up a bit, I would love to meet you in person, maybe for a nice dinner or some live jazz music. Until then, I hope we can keep the conversation going here. That way, once we finally do meet, it'll feel as if we already know one another. That said, it's lights-out for me as the alarm is set for a 4:00 a.m. training session at the gym. Have a wonderful night, gorgeous. Looking forward to hearing from you again soon...xx, Shane

Nia's pulse began to throb as she reread the message. She debated whether to respond now or wait until the morning. After a mental back-and-forth, she decided to hold off so as not to appear too eager.

The minute she set her cell down, thoughts of the investigation crept back into her head.

Enough, Nia told herself. She'd dedicated enough of her day to the case. It was time to focus on something a little more pleasant—like the message exchange with Shane.

Thanks to him, her evening was ending on a high note. "So let's keep it there," she murmured, grabbing her phone and scrolling through his photos once again.

Chapter Seven

Drew floored the accelerator, flying across Sparrow Lane Bridge, then tearing down Candlewood Avenue. He tried Nia's cell again. The call went straight to voicemail.

"Nia," he huffed. "I've been trying to reach you for the past hour. I hope you're getting my calls and texts. I need you out at Latimer Park. *Now.* A couple of joggers found a dead body on a bench over by the duck pond. Chief Mitchell and the forensic team should already be there. I'm pulling up now. Call me when you get this message."

After parking along a side street near the tennis courts, he sprinted across the freshly cut grass. Panic swirled through his lungs as he choked on shallow breaths of air.

It was a little past six-thirty in the morning—too early for the recreational areas to be occupied. *Thank God.* The last thing Juniper PD needed was for people to catch sight of the gruesome scene.

Yellowish-orange light broke through dark clouds as the sun began to rise. A few of the officers who'd worked the overnight shift were already there, wrapping yellow Police Line tape around lodgepole pine tree trunks. In the center of it all was a shallow duck pond. Birds were splashing about, their fluttering wings flipping over banana water lilies in response to all the commotion.

On a black wrought-iron bench right across from the

water sat a woman's body. Her head was slumped over, and just like Katie Douglas, her throat had been slashed. Blood drenched her off-white bomber jacket. Her hands and feet were bound with duct tape. And a piece of paper was stuffed inside her right hand.

"Hey, Taylor!" Officer Davis called out. "I just got a text from the chief. He should be here any minute. Any word from Officer Brooks?"

"No, not yet. I've sent several messages and left voice-mails. Her phone must be out of juice because she never turns it off."

The thought of something happening to Nia flashed through Drew's mind. *Don't do that,* he told himself, gritting his teeth in frustration.

As he approached the victim, Drew's grip on the evidence collection kit tightened, his stomach turning at the grisly sight. The woman looked to be no older than twenty-five. A long dark braid hung down her back. From what he could tell, her height and weight appeared to be almost identical to Katie's. The similarities between the two crime scenes were uncanny. Either they were dealing with a copycat killer, or their suspect had struck again.

"So what do you think?" Officer Davis asked. "Is it possible we might have a serial killer on our hands?"

"Not only is it possible, but in my opinion, it's highly likely. And apparently he's got a type. Notice the parallels between this victim and the last?"

"Yeah, I do. You know who else comes to mind when I compare the two?"

"Let me guess. Linda Echols."

"You got it."

Staring down at the ground, Officer Davis dug his heel into a clump of grass before emitting a forced cough. "Hey, uh...Officer Taylor? There's something I need to say to you. I feel terrible after insisting that Chief Mitchell take me off the park surveillance job. You're the lead investigator on this case, and I should've listened to you and believed that hunch you were feeling about the clue left at the last crime scene. You knew it might lead to something like this. But I got impatient. Blew it off, thinking the killer was playing some sick game rather than tipping us off."

"Actually, it was Officer Brooks who was adamant that we keep watch on the park. I just wish I'd been more aggressive in trying to convince Chief Mitchell to change his mind. But the reality is neither of us can do anything about what's happened here. What we *can* do is put every effort into catching this maniac before he kills again."

"Agreed." Shoving his hands in his pockets, Officer Davis slowly backed away. "But I just can't shake the guilt of knowing this victim's blood is on my hands. I could've prevented this. From here on out, trust that I've got your back and will follow your lead until we get this case solved."

"Thanks, Davis. I appreciate you saying that."

"Officer Taylor!"

The sight of Nia running toward Drew eased his tense shoulders.

"Hey, where have you been? I was starting to worry about you."

"I'm so sorry I didn't call you back," she panted. "My phone battery died right after your first text came through. So what's the latest? Are the joggers still here? Have they been questioned yet?"

"They were questioned briefly by responding officers but weren't able to offer up much info. I'd like for us to interview them more thoroughly down at the station."

Drew followed Nia's gaze as she pointed toward the

street. "The medical examiner just pulled up. I'd better slip into some protective gear before we get started. I'll be right back."

As he watched Nia hurry off, Officer Davis nudged Drew's shoulder.

"What's up?" Drew asked him.

"Yeah, that's my question to you. What's up?"

"What do you mean?"

Nodding in Nia's direction, Officer Davis replied, "What's going on between you and Brooks? I noticed how quickly your mood lifted the second she ran over here."

Drew's eyes narrowed at the officer's sly smirk. "I'm just glad to know she's all right after not hearing back from her earlier."

"You sure that's all it is?"

"Yeah. I'm positive." Drew broke the officer's inquisitive stare and pulled on a mask and gloves. "Look, we need to get started on the crime scene analysis while the medical examiner processes the body. I wanna move on that ASAP so I can take a look at whatever's inside the victim's hand."

With a slow nod, Officer Davis caught the hint and dropped the subject. "You got it, boss."

DREW EASED INTO a seat inside Earl's Steakhouse and waited for Nia to arrive at the table. She'd been stopped near the entrance by a group of old friends from college. After being introduced, he had stood around waiting as the girl talk commenced. But once they began discussing bridal showers and TikTok makeup tutorials, he excused himself and followed the hostess to their booth.

After he and Nia had spent the day processing the crime scene, Drew offered to treat her to dinner. Sending her home alone straight from the station just didn't feel right. As her

mentor, he wanted to make sure she was okay and offer up a
little moral support over a nice steak and glass of cabernet.

Drew peered over the top of the menu, watching as Nia's
friends fawned all over her. Whatever she was saying had
them completely captivated. Nia had that effect on people
wherever they went. When she walked into a room, everyone took notice. Whenever she spoke, those around her
stopped and listened. Nia was a natural-born leader who had
that *it* factor. Her beauty only added to her appeal. The more
she and Drew worked together, the deeper his admiration
grew. And if he were being honest, his attraction as well.

The moment she pivoted and headed toward the table,
Drew dropped his head, diverting his attention back to
the wine list. Before doing so, he caught a glimpse of her
fading smile. There was a look of agony behind her tired
eyes. He wasn't surprised, considering they'd spent hours
at Latimer Park, scouring the crime scene for evidence.
This being Nia's first encounter with a murder victim, her
discomfort showed—the slight gagging, watering eyes and
excessive fidgeting. He'd recommended she work on com-
pleting the police report while he processed the scene. But
she refused, insisting she was fine.

Drew appreciated Nia's endurance as she ended up being
an essential part of the analysis. She was the one who had
initiated the fingerprint search, dusting the bench with a
dark powder and using clear adhesive tape to lift the prints.
She'd spotted a muddy shoeprint near the victim's feet that
the other officers missed. To record that pattern, she and
Drew used a sheet of rubber layered in gelatin to lift it off
the soil's surface. And then there was the cigarette butt Nia
had found floating near the edge of the duck pond that she'd
retrieved before the birds got to it.

It was quite a rousing sight, watching the awe on their

colleagues' faces as they observed Nia's work. They'd never seen her in action since this was her first time processing an active crime scene. Drew on the other hand was accustomed to her procedural acumen. But even he was impressed when she immediately recognized the pattern on the shoeprint. It contained the same beveled edge treading as the Lacrosse hunting boot impression found at Katie Douglas's crime scene—convincing both officers that the women had been killed by the same perpetrator.

"Hey," Nia breathed, pulling Drew from his thoughts as she slid into the seat across from him. "Sorry about that. I haven't seen some of those women in years. We had a lot to catch up on. But anyway, thanks again for suggesting this. I cannot tell you how much I needed it."

"Of course. It's the least I could do considering all the great work you put in today. Plus I still owed you after our coffee outing."

"Oh, please. With the amount of wine I'm about to drink? You'll wish you would've covered the coffee date instead—" She froze, a deep shade of crimson coloring her cheeks. "I'm sorry. But did I just refer to our mentoring meeting as a *date*?"

"Yes," he replied, chuckling at her horrified reaction. "I believe you did."

Her mouth fell open, but no words were spoken as she began fanning her face with the specials menu.

"Hey," Drew murmured, flashing a relaxed smile. "It was just a little slipup. Actually it was more like a welcome faux pas. We needed something to take the heaviness off of the day."

Nia's tense expression softened. Reaching across the table, she gave his hand a squeeze, her fingertips teasing his palm. "You're right. Because today was definitely a lot to deal with."

He barely heard her as a tingling sensation shot up his arm. When it snaked below his belt Drew straightened up, turning his attention back to the menu. "So...anything look good?"

"Everything looks good. And I didn't eat a thing today. I'm actually surprised I have an appetite after seeing..."

"Are you okay?" Drew asked after her voice trailed off.

"Yep," she quickly replied, forcing a tight grin before burying her face in the menu. But he could still see the creases of worry lining her forehead. "I'm thinking of getting the barbecue-glazed salmon with a side of garlic mashed potatoes and roasted asparagus. What about you?"

"I'm going with the bone-in rib eye, loaded baked potato and spring sweet peas."

"*Aaand* I've got that," someone chimed in.

Drew's head swiveled, not realizing the server had approached. After taking the rest of their orders, she rushed off just as the officers' cell phones pinged. Drew grabbed his first.

"Oh, good. We've got an ID on the victim. Her name is Violet Shields. Twenty-six years old. Her parents identified the body at the medical examiner's office."

Biting down on her bottom lip, Nia's eyes remained stuck to her screen.

"Did you receive this text as well?" he asked her.

"No, mine is from Dawn at Latimer Park. And it's not good news. She reviewed last night's surveillance footage. The cameras captured the basketball and tennis courts and the playground. But nothing near the duck pond."

"*Dammit.* I wonder if there's footage of anyone walking past those areas. Unless the suspect entered the park through the back area near the trees, Dawn should've seen him making his way toward the pond."

"You're right. I've already asked that she forward the footage to us so we can review it ourselves, but I'll remind her to do that now."

Drew paused when a server approached with their wood-grilled octopus and drinks. Once she was out of earshot, he said, "Hey, there's something else I want to talk to you about."

"Okay..." Nia uttered. "I'm listening."

"I was talking with Officer Davis this morning before you arrived at the crime scene. He mentioned how much he regretted removing himself from the Latimer Park surveillance assignment. So on behalf of him, myself *and* Chief Mitchell, I wanna apologize."

"Drew, you don't have to—"

"No, no, I do. We really dropped the ball on that. You were the one who initially made that suggestion, and you were one hundred percent right. Had the department taken heed, maybe Violet's murder could've been avoided. So, moving forward, just know that I'll push harder for what you want. Because obviously your instincts are a hell of a lot stronger than some of these veteran cops."

"Thank you for that, Drew. But like I was going to say, there's no need for you to apologize. It wasn't your decision. It started with Officer Davis and ended with Chief Mitchell."

"True." He took a sip of his whiskey sour while Nia filled their plates with octopus. The gesture warmed him, sparking memories of what it felt like being out on a date. The fire it incited within his gut. The excitement, the anticipation of what would come later.

Everything you shouldn't be feeling for Nia...

"Drew?"

"Yep?" he uttered, so buried in his thoughts that he hadn't noticed her handing him a plate.

"Where did you go just now? It seemed like you faded out or something."

"Oh, sorry. I, uh… I was just thinking about Officer Davis," he lied. "And how he swore to never make a rash decision that could cost someone their life again."

"Good. Hey, switching topics for a quick sec. How's Tim doing?"

"He's doing well. Better than the doctors expected, actually. He's out of the ICU, and so far, there are no signs of any brain damage. They're not sure how much longer he'll be in the hospital, but afterwards I'm pretty sure he's going to have a lengthy stint in rehab. They keep saying he's lucky to be alive."

"Any new leads on the driver of the car that hit him?"

"No, unfortunately. Tim didn't get a look at it. And since the accident occurred on a rural road where there were no houses, we weren't able to obtain any surveillance footage." Drew rammed his fork into a tentacle. "I don't know why, but something is telling me that accident was intentional."

"Meaning?"

"I'm wondering if Tim was targeted. And whether the crash is connected to this murder investigation. Because it happened right after Katie Douglas's body was found. Could it have been the killer's way of trying to throw us off, and leave the department with one less officer on the case?"

"Could be. At this point, I wouldn't count any theory out." Nia swiped open her cell and pulled up a photo. "We haven't had a chance to discuss the clue left inside the victim's hand at Latimer Park. What do you make of it?"

Drew studied the image of the wedding invitation Nia had snapped at the crime scene. The thick cream pearlescent stock and gold print was smeared with blood. But he was still able to make out the wording. At the top were two initials, *T* and *I*. The names of the couple set to exchange vows, Terrance Gauff and Ingrid Porter, were printed underneath. The wedding location was at the bottom—the Charlie Sifford Country Club.

"Well, I definitely think it's alluding to what our killer has planned next. And I bet we're on the same page regarding next steps."

"What—that we should set up surveillance at the club?"

"Exactly. Which is why I already spoke to Chief Mitchell and he assigned Officer Ryan to the job. He's patrolling the place as we speak."

Nia held her glass in the air. "Now *that* is some good news I needed to hear. Cheers."

Tapping his glass against hers, Drew's gaze lingered on Nia until the server approached with their food.

"You know what I suggest we do?" Drew asked. "Pause all talk of the investigation and enjoy our dinner."

"Yes, good idea."

Drew eyed her plate, adding, "You know what else would be a good idea? Sliding a piece of that salmon onto my plate."

"Oh, really now," Nia retorted, pointing her fork toward his entrée. "How about we make a trade? A slice of my salmon for a piece of your steak?"

"Deal."

As Drew cut into his rib eye, the tension in his shoulders slackened, which he credited to the change of subject. But underneath that theory lay the fact that Nia's presence had put him at ease.

Yet while the case discussion had ended, thoughts of the investigation persisted. The wedding invitation left at the scene was a stark reminder that the clock was ticking. And it was only a matter of time before the killer would strike again.

Chapter Eight

Nia pulled into the driveway of her tri-level townhome and willed her fatigued legs to carry her to the door. The day had been exhausting—both physically and emotionally. Dinner with Drew did lighten the load of the investigation. But by the end of the meal, she was fighting to keep her eyes open. He'd insisted on ordering key lime pie for dessert, which only exacerbated her exhaustion. Now that Nia was finally home, climbing into bed was the only thing on her mind.

Nia stopped at the mailbox on the way in. Just as she opened the lid, a light flickered inside the house.

She hesitated, peering through the canted bay window's sheer curtains. Every light in the living room was off. Yet the kitchen light was on.

But...how?

She could've sworn she'd turned it off that morning.

You're just tired. You rushed out to the crime scene before 6:00 a.m. Probably left the light on by accident...

Grabbing the stack of envelopes from the mailbox, Nia made her way inside. She kicked off her boots, switched on a lamp and shuffled through the mail.

"Bill, bill, junk, another bill—"

She froze when the last envelope came into view. It didn't have her full name on it, nor her address. The letters *NIA* were handwritten across the middle in bold black letters.

"What the hell is this?"

She tore open the envelope and snatched a thick cream pearlescent card from it. Scanned the beautiful gold print, then dropped it to the floor. Her hands shook as she bent down to pick it up.

It can't be. You're just seeing things...

But upon further inspection, Nia realized her eyes weren't deceiving her. In her hand was an invitation to Ingrid Porter and Terrance Gauff's wedding—the same invitation they'd found at the crime scene. And in the lower left-hand corner was a bloody fingerprint.

"No, no, no..." she muttered.

Nia grabbed her purse, almost ripping the zipper trying to get to her cell phone. With trembling fingers she fumbled through the call log and dialed Drew's number. The call went straight to voicemail.

"Drew! Call me as soon as you get this. I got a wedding invitation in the mail today that matches the one we found at Latimer Park—"

The kitchen light went out again.

Her phone fell by her side. She glanced at the alarm control panel hanging by the door. It had been disabled.

What the...

Terror grabbed hold of Nia's joints as she stumbled against the wall. Without taking her eyes off the kitchen entrance, she reached down and pulled her gun from her purse.

Stay calm. This is what you were trained to do.

Standing straight up, Nia pointed her weapon toward the doorway. "Hey! Whoever's in here, just so you know, I am a police officer. I am armed. And I *will* shoot you. So come out into the living room with your hands up!"

Silence.

She ducked down while inching along the back of the couch. "This is your final warning. Trust me, this is not a game." Curling her finger around the trigger, Nia yelled, "Either come out, or I will—"

"Don't shoot!"

The kitchen suddenly lit up.

"Who the hell is that?" Nia called out right before her sister, Ivy, came bouncing into the living room.

"Niaaa! Hey, girl! Oh, how I've missed you, *seesto*!"

"Ivy! What are you doing here? And why would you scare me half to death like that? I almost shot you!"

"Come on, now. You weren't gonna shoot me."

"The hell I wasn't!"

Ivy jumped into her arms, ending the rant as her wild curls smothered Nia's entire face. Typical Ivy—showering her sister with love to deflect from the issue at hand.

"Anyway, I've missed you, too," Nia said, relenting, before she embraced her sister. But as she grabbed hold of Ivy's bony back, she quickly pulled away. "Wait, what's going on with you? Why do you feel so tiny?"

"Because I *am* tiny." Holding her scrawny arms out at her sides, Ivy spun a three-sixty, showing off the skintight black pleather dress clinging to her rail-thin figure. "I've lost fifteen pounds since the last time you saw me."

"Yeah, well, the problem is you didn't need to lose any weight. Whatever look you've got going on isn't healthy."

"Have you forgotten that I'm in the entertainment industry? You know how it is. The thinner you are, the bigger your chances of becoming a star."

Nia watched through worried eyes as her sister flitted back into the kitchen. Ivy, also known as the black sheep of the Brooks family, had a checkered past that plagued her for years. She'd hung out with a rough crowd during high school and had gotten herself into trouble on numerous occasions.

Those incidents of stealing from local stores for fun, vandalizing the property of people who'd allegedly wronged her and being caught drinking after hours at Latimer Park had left a stain on her reputation. After barely graduating, she'd run off to Los Angeles to pursue a singing career. She and Nia had managed to remain close over the years. But Ivy's erratic behavior remained a point of contention in their relationship.

"So," Ivy said, bouncing back inside the living room with two glasses of wine, "what have I missed since I've been gone?"

"First of all, I don't need another glass of wine. I had plenty during dinner."

"Oh? Dinner with who? Someone special you haven't told me about?"

Plopping down on the couch, Nia replied, "Nope. Just a coworker."

"Hmm," Ivy purred, sliding into the spot next to her. "That's what your mouth says, but that glimmer in your eyes is telling a completely different story. Spill the tea, sis! Tell me all about him."

"There's nothing to tell. Like I said, he's a coworker." When Ivy handed her a glass, Nia turned away. "No, please. Trust me, I've had enough. All I need at this point is a glass of ice water and my bed. I am exhausted. Speaking of which, I wish you would've told me you were coming to town. I wouldn't have stayed out so late."

"Don't worry. There will be plenty of time for us to spend together since you'll be seeing a whole lot more of me."

"What do you mean?"

"Well…" Ivy avoided Nia's eyes as she picked at a rogue

thread hanging from her hemline. "I don't know exactly when I'm going back to LA. So I'll be here for a while."

Judging by the look of Ivy's pouty lower lip, Nia knew what that meant. Ivy was running from something.

"Where are you staying? With mom and dad?"

Suddenly, Ivy's scowl curled into a sugary sweet grin. "That's what I wanted to talk to you about. I was hoping that maybe I could, you know..."

"Oh, no," Nia interrupted, shaking her head so adamantly that her gold hoops slapped her cheeks. "Absolutely not. I was just assigned to a *huge* case that could make or break my career. I do not have time to keep an eye on you."

"Why would you have to keep an eye on me?"

"*Please.* Is that even a real question? Or should I pull up your police report and remind you of all the mess you've gotten yourself into over the years?"

"Can you please stop throwing that up in my face? All that happened forever ago. I'm not the girl I used to be. I've grown up."

Crossing her arms over her stomach, Nia watched as Ivy guzzled her wine, then picked up the second glass she'd poured. "So, tell me, what brought you back to Juniper?"

"I just needed a break. You know how LA can be. Hectic. Grueling. *Expensive*. Plus I got tired of the whole auditioning grind. Singing my heart out day after day, week after week, while working my ass off to make ends meet was getting old. Even though I'd land a few small gigs here and there, they weren't getting me anywhere."

As Ivy slouched down farther into the couch, Nia suspected she wasn't telling the whole truth. Her sister was known to be secretive. She'd always been a wild card, making spontaneous decisions without thinking of the repercussions. So the abrupt move back home didn't come as much of a surprise.

"Well, you should know that now isn't the best time to be in Juniper," Nia warned.

"Why not?"

"Haven't you seen the news? We've got a serial killer on the loose."

"Wait, you've got a *what*?"

Nia tossed her hand in the air for extra emphasis. "There is a serial killer hunting down women in Juniper. He's binding their wrists and ankles, slashing their throats and leaving their bodies on display in public places."

"Oh my God," Ivy moaned, covering her mouth in disgust. "That is…that is *sick*."

"Yes, it is. And I'm assisting the lead investigator on the case—"

"Wait, *you*? But how? You're still a rookie. You just made it onto the force."

"It's a long story. Look, my point is, this partner of mine is a hard-nosed veteran who's working the biggest case of his career, too, and he's depending on me. So I don't have time to be looking after you and making sure you're staying out of trouble."

"And you won't have to," Ivy insisted. "I've already reconnected with several old friends, so if I need anything, I can go to them. Plus I landed a job bartending at the Bullseye Bar and Grill. So I'll be fine."

"Oh, so you told everybody you'd be in town except for me? Even though *I'm* the one you want to stay with?"

Giving Nia's thigh a playful pinch, Ivy squealed, "Yes! Thanks again for letting me crash here."

"Yeah, yeah. Just make sure you stay out of trouble."

Ivy suddenly grew quiet while staring down into her

glass. Watching as her sister's eyes filled with tears, Nia didn't interpret the mood switch as a sentimental sign of missing home. It was something deeper. Something troubling.

Knowing Ivy, the more Nia probed, the more she'd withdraw. So Nia decided to leave it be, at least for the time being. She was completely drained. The talk could wait until tomorrow.

"Listen," Nia said, brushing Ivy's bangs out of her eyes. "I'm gonna need for you to be careful. I haven't forgotten about those old friends of yours and how they operate. They weren't the best people. And from what I hear, they've only gotten worse. More importantly, with this killer on the loose, I don't like the idea of you running around town and bartending until the early hours of the morning. Things have changed since you left."

"As hard as it is for you to grasp this fact, I can take care of myself. Stop worrying so much. I'll be fine."

Before Nia could respond, Ivy drained the second glass of wine, then hopped up from the couch.

"Wait, where are you going?"

"To change clothes. I'm getting together with the girls tonight. They're throwing me a little impromptu welcome home party at Army and Lou's Jazz Club. You wanna come?"

"Absolutely not. It's already late and I have to be back at the station early in the morning. How are you getting there?"

Pressing her hands together, Ivy pleaded, "I was hoping you'd let me borrow your car. *Pleeease?*"

"No, ma'am. I highly doubt that you'd bring it back in time for me to make it to work. Can't one of your friends pick you up?"

"I guess one of them will have to, won't they?"

"I guess so."

"Fine," Ivy huffed, charging up the staircase. "I'll call Madison. Oh, and nice way to welcome your baby sister home."

"Maybe the welcome would've been much nicer had my baby sister told me she'd be here instead of breaking into my house and scaring the hell out of me."

"It's not breaking in when I used the key you gave me!"

"It is when I don't even know you're in town!"

The sound of Ivy's silver cowboy boots pounding the stairs grew louder in response. Nia ignored it and turned on the television, now wide awake thanks to her sister's unexpected arrival.

A flash of sparkly cream cardstock caught Nia's eye. She shot to her feet and ran to the console table by the door. After being startled by Ivy, she'd forgotten all about the wedding invitation left inside her mailbox. Nia had also forgotten about Drew, who'd yet to call her back.

She checked the cell. No text notification from him either. She tried calling again. The call went straight to voicemail.

Dammit.

Nia left another message, snapped a photo of the invitation and texted it to Drew. Once the message was sent, she dead-bolted the door and grabbed her gun off the table. Just as she set the alarm, her phone rang. It was him.

"Are you okay?" he asked the second she picked up. "I got your voicemail and saw that text. What is going on?"

"*A lot.* I'm fine though. A little shaken up, but I'm okay."

"Good. Sorry it took so long to call you back. I stopped by the gym on the way home because after the day we had, I needed to get in a workout. I didn't realize my phone was on silent. But about that invitation. First of all, do you need for me to come over there? Because I can—"

"No, Drew. You don't have to do that. It's late. And I know you're tired. Plus I've got my Glock right here next to me."

"Okay. Well, if that changes, just let me know. I'm sure getting that invitation was disturbing to say the least. Assuming it was left by the killer, that means he knows where you live. And with that being said, are you *sure* you don't want me to come—"

"I'm positive," Nia interrupted once again, hating the idea of being a burden.

"Look, do me a favor. Put the invitation inside a plastic bag and bring it to the station tomorrow. We'll send it to the crime lab first thing and have it tested for DNA."

"I will." Nia paused at the sound of a glass crashing to the floor right above her head. "Oh God…"

"Wait, what was that I just heard?"

"My sister is upstairs destroying my house."

"Ivy's in town? I didn't know she was coming to visit."

"Yeah, neither did I. When I got home she was already here and scared the crap out of me."

"Nia!" Ivy screamed from the top of the landing. "Do you have any hair mousse?"

"No, I do not!"

Drew's throaty chuckle floated through her ear.

"What's so funny?"

"You and your sister, sounding like two teenagers."

"Interesting you should say that. Because she's acting like a teenager, asking to borrow my car and whatnot. I'm still trying to figure out what she's doing back in Juniper. I have a feeling she's keeping something from me. I'll get it out of her eventually."

"Does she know about this homicidal predator out here roaming the streets?"

"She does now. But Ivy's the type who thinks nothing will happen to her. She's already got me worrying. Especially after hearing that she'll be bartending at Bullseye."

"Look, you've got enough on your plate. I don't want your blood pressure to go up because you're stressing over your sister. I'll talk to the guys and ask them to keep an eye on the bar during her shifts."

"Drew, that is a lot to ask. Are you sure it wouldn't be too much trouble?"

"I'm positive."

"Thank you," she murmured, her quiet tone buzzing with warmth. "I really appreciate it."

"Of course. Oh, and before I forget, I heard back from the joggers who found the victim's body at Latimer Park. They're going to come in tomorrow morning and talk with us. I don't know how useful it'll be since they didn't see much. But sometimes when these witnesses are questioned at the station, they suddenly remember things they'd initially forgotten."

"Good to know. Let's hope that's the case." Nia hesitated when Ivy came clomping down the stairs. "Listen, I'd better go. My sister is getting ready to leave, and I need to give her one more lecture before she heads out."

"Yes, please do. If anything comes up, call me. And don't forget to keep your gun close. Unless you decide otherwise, I'll see you in the morning."

Nia sat there, contemplating whether or not she *should* decide otherwise.

You'd better not. Between all that wine you drank and your vulnerable state, there's no telling what you might do if he comes over...

"Thanks, Drew. I'll see you in the morning."

"Yeah, um…see you then."

There was a tinge of disappointment in his low tone. Nia wondered if it stemmed from his desire to be there with her or the fact that he was just tired. He disconnected the call before she could inquire.

"Okay," Ivy said, strutting into the living room as if she were on a catwalk. "What do you think?"

Nia looked up from her phone and almost fell off the couch. "What in the world are you wearing?" she asked, glaring at the sheer black negligee and glittery platform heels.

"*What?* I think I look good! And according to my nine thousand-plus followers on TikTok, they think so too."

A flash of anger shot through Nia as her sister snapped several selfies. "You aren't taking any of the warnings I gave seriously, are you?"

"Of course I am! I already told my girls about the investigation. Madison is planning on covering the case on her YouTube channel. Oh! And she wanted me to ask if you'd be willing to do an interview with her. You know, on behalf of the Juniper PD. Maybe that partner you mentioned could go live with her, too. Ooh, and what about your boss? Chief Marshall, or whatever his name is."

"It's Chief Mitchell. And, no. None of us are going on some YouTube channel to discuss the case. Besides, I thought Madison's channel was all about makeup and fitness."

"It is. But true crime is really hot right now. A lot of vloggers are doing this thing where they apply their makeup while covering cases. You've gotta keep up, big sis."

A loud engine roared out front.

"Maddy's here!" Ivy exclaimed, teetering toward the

door to the beat of a blaring horn. Right before Ivy stepped outside, Nia grabbed her arm.

"Hey, listen. You need to be careful. Keep your eyes open and call me if anything comes up. Don't go wandering off by yourself or get too friendly with every person you see. Most importantly, please don't do anything illegal."

"Yes, *mother*. Now wish me luck. It's open mic night and the winner gets five hundred dollars."

"Good luck. Oh, and try not to stay out all night!"

"Bye!"

As Ivy went bouncing toward a red Toyota Supra, Nia stepped onto the porch and waved. She could barely hear Madison scream her name over the loud house music.

Worry pricked her skin watching the pair speed off into the night.

She's grown, Nia reminded herself. *She'll be fine...*

The night air was cool. And eerily peaceful. Nia eyed the broadleaf evergreen shrubs lining her rock garden, imagining some stranger audaciously invading her space.

The killer had dropped an ominous hint. He wanted her to know that he was aware of her connection to the case. Leaving the invitation was his attempt to extinguish her efforts. But it wasn't going to work. If anything, it would serve as fuel to further ignite her drive.

When she stepped back inside the house, a thought dropped in Nia's head like a hammer to a nail—security cameras were mounted over her front and back doors.

How could you forget that?

She threw her head back in relief and glanced at the top of the door.

"What the…"

The security camera was gone.

Nia rushed inside the house and bolted the door, then

grabbed her phone. This time when she dialed Drew's number, he picked up on the first ring.

"Hey, what's up?" he asked. "Is everything okay?"

"No, everything is not okay. I need for you to come to my place. *Now.*"

Chapter Nine

Drew flicked a packet of raw sugar inside his coffee and stared across the conference room table. Nia's distraught expression pained him. The investigation was not going as he'd hoped. And now that she had become a target, it felt as though he was failing her.

The DNA evidence found at Latimer Park matched the evidence from Shelby's Candy Factory. Yet law enforcement still couldn't figure out the suspect's identity since no match had turned up in the national database.

The interview with joggers who'd discovered Violet Shields's body was a complete bust. Not only did they have nothing to report from the crime scene, but they'd brought their children into the station hoping they could tour the facility.

Surveillance footage saved to Nia's computer from the day the wedding invitation had been delivered didn't reveal much. The suspect had not come fully into view after crossing the neighbor's lawn and creeping up onto the porch from the side railing.

From what the officers could tell, he appeared slender and was dressed in all black. A mask covered his face and his head and shoulders were hunched over, making him unrecognizable. The steel rod swinging from his hand, however, was visible. Once he'd reached the landing, the camera shook violently before it went crashing to the ground. Nia's neighbors had allowed her to view their security footage. But none of their cameras were positioned to capture images of her house.

Despite his coffee being steaming hot, Drew took a long sip. The bitter burn on his tongue somehow cancelled the frustration brewing in his chest. The conference room table was covered with every piece of evidence they had collected. He'd suggested they start back at square one and work their way through each crime scene in hopes of stumbling upon something they'd missed. So far, both he and Nia had come up empty.

"This is so aggravating," she said, fiddling with the cap on her water bottle. "All these reports, all the photos, the DNA evidence… But still no suspects. The biggest disappointment was that bloody fingerprint found on the wedding invitation inside my mailbox. I just knew it would link us to our suspect."

"Yeah, same. The fact that it belonged to Violet Shields was just another sinister way for the killer to taunt us. What about that Someone for Everyone app? Have you heard back from the administrator?"

"No, not yet." Nia grabbed her phone and swiped it open. "But I'll check again, just to see if something came through since the last time I looked. I'll also do some online digging to find out who the owners are and get in touch with them directly."

"Good idea. While you do that, I'll have Officer Ryan work on getting a subpoena. That way they'll be forced to hand over the information whether they want to or not. We've waited long enough for a response, which is ridiculous considering our request pertains to a criminal investigation…"

Drew's voice trailed off as Nia smiled at her phone screen.

"What's got you grinning over there like a giddy schoolgirl?"

"Nothing!" She fumbled her cell before sliding it to the side. "I was just—just checking on that response from the administrator."

"Any word from them?"

"Nope. No word yet."

Nia's bottle almost slipped from her hand. She caught it just in time, but not before a stream of water trickled onto the table. Quickly wiping it up with her sleeve, she snatched a report and pointed at the notes. "I've been meaning to ask about Violet's cell phone. Any luck tracking it down?"

"Not as of yet."

Drew watched as Nia's attention remained on the document. He hadn't known her for long. But he knew her well enough to realize when something was off. And she'd been acting strange all morning.

"Hey, is everything all right?"

"Yeah," she uttered a beat too soon. "Everything's fine. Why?"

"You just seem a bit…distracted. Is it that wedding invitation or your security camera going missing? Or what about your sister? I know you were caught off guard after the way she dropped in unexpectedly."

Finally looking up at him, Nia replied, "*Yes.* That's it. I think the fact that Ivy came storming back into town like a tornado has thrown me for a loop. But again, I'm fine. Thanks for asking. Anyway, back to Violet's cell phone. Does her family think they may be able to find it?"

Drew could smell her lie from across the table. Clearly

Ivy's visit had nothing to do with the joy on Nia's face after she'd checked the dating app. He was dying to ask what she was hiding. But it was none of his business. Not to mention he shouldn't even be concerned.

So why do you care?

Ignoring the annoying voice in his head, Drew said, "Violet's family is on top of the search for her cell. They're gonna try and track it down inside her house which, according to them, is a bit of a mess since she had some hoarding tendencies. I've also contacted her phone provider. So even if we can't get our hands on the actual device I'll have a record of her activity."

"Good. Because there is the chance that the killer took it. I'm guessing Violet didn't share her phone's location with anyone?"

"Nope. Nor did she utilize the Find My Device feature. And that's part of the problem. The more I've spoken with her family, the more I realize just how private of a person she was. According to her father, she was also dealing with issues of paranoia. Violet was convinced that if she used any sort of tracking technology, people outside of her family and friend circle would be able to trace her whereabouts."

Nia clicked her tongue while flipping through the photos of Violet's crime scene. "And what ends up happening? Someone still managed to hunt her down and kill her." Stopping on a close-up of the victim's slashed throat, she glared at it, then shoved the whole stack inside the folder. "Where do we go from here, Drew?"

"Great question…"

He rocked back in his black ergonomic chair and scanned the piles strewn in front of him. The documents became a blur of chaos as his mind sought out an answer.

When he leaned his elbows onto the table, Drew's laptop awoke from sleep mode. Katie Douglas's Facebook page popped up. He reached over and enlarged her profile picture. She stared back at him, her head tilted toward the sun while throwing up a peace sign.

"That picture is so haunting," Nia said. "Katie looks so happy and vibrant. And *alive*. To look at her there, knowing she's dead now, is just—just so disturbing."

"Yes, it is…"

Nia's words sparked a fire in Drew that pushed him away from the table.

"I got it," he said, pounding his fist into his palm.

"I'm sorry. You what?"

"I got it! I've got the answer. You and I are going to print out photos of Katie and take them down to Shelby's Candy Factory."

"And do what? Hang them up in hopes that someone will recognize her? I don't know how effective that'll be considering the place is abandoned. And the people who hang out there aren't the type to wanna assist law enforcement."

"Here's what I'm thinking. First we'll use social media to get some intel on when the next underground rave is happening. Once we find out, we'll show up with Katie's photo in hand and ask the attendees about her. Maybe she used to hang out there. Who knows, the killer may even hang out there. Either way, the answers we're looking for might be with the people who party at that factory."

Grabbing her notebook and flipping it open, Nia said, "I like that idea. I like it a lot. On another note, you mentioning a rave brought the whole use of illegal substances to mind, which made me think of the victims' toxicology reports. Have the results come back?"

"No, not yet. But I'm curious to know whether any of

them were drugged. I'll put in a call to the medical examiner's office once we're done here and find out when we can expect them. As for now," he continued, pulling up his email, "I'm gonna send Officer Ryan a message asking if he's got intel on the next rave since he's usually up on those types of events."

"You know who else might know something? Ivy. I wouldn't be surprised if some of her old friends were the ones throwing them. I'll shoot her a text now."

As Nia typed away on her phone, Drew peered across the table, taking in her natural beauty. While it was on full display, there was something different. Her eyes, usually sparkling with enthusiasm, appeared dull, almost lifeless. Her lips were never without some shade of gloss. Today, they were bare. While she was still giving her all to the investigation, that fire and drive were missing, as if her spirit had been broken.

"Hey, Brooks," he said, trying his best to sound casual, "how are you holding up?"

Her fingers froze over the phone screen. "What do you mean?"

Those fluttering eyelids indicated that she knew exactly what he'd meant. Drew was slow to respond, empathizing with Nia as he thought back on his days as a rookie cop. They hadn't been easy. The need to appear tough overrode moments of vulnerability. He'd seen Nia the night that invitation showed up in her mailbox and the security camera went missing. She had been damn near inconsolable, falling into his arms the moment he stepped through the door.

But now, as she sat in front of him at the station, Nia was struggling to appear resilient, as if she wasn't being affected by the case. He needed her to know that she didn't have to put up a front for him. Their relationship was a safe space—a soft place to land when everything around her hardened.

"You know," he began, his husky tone laced with sincerity, "you don't have to put on an act for me. You've been through a lot. It's okay to be open and show emotion. You may be a police officer, but you're also human. I just need to know that you're all right. If you're not, I wanna do everything in my power to get you there. I can put a patrol car on duty to keep an eye on your house twenty-four seven. Hell, I'll even stay with you for the time being if that's what it'll take to make you feel secure."

Slowly setting her phone aside, Nia blew a heavy sigh. Her body shifted as she finally looked him in the eyes. "Thank you, Drew. Honestly? I am still shaken up. I don't even go into the kitchen to get a glass of water without taking my gun with me. But I'm working through it. At this point I'm more concerned about Ivy. She's the one who's constantly running around town, coming in at all hours of the night. I've talked her into carrying a can of pepper spray everywhere she goes, so that's made me feel a little better. And the camera your friend installed has helped ease my anxiety, too, so…"

"So, you're hanging in there?"

"Yes. I'm hanging in there." Her pursed lips spread into a faint smile. "I appreciate you looking out for me."

Drew's chest pulled at her gratitude. It was confirmation that his words of encouragement were well received. Nia's response deepened his need to protect her, triggering a surge of emotions that fueled his burgeoning attraction.

Pull back…

He downed a swallow of coffee before grabbing his phone. "I should call the medical examiner's office. Get an update on those toxicology reports."

As he dialed the number, Nia's cell pinged. Her face lit up after checking the notification. A twinge of jealousy stirred in Drew's gut as he wondered what sparked the wave of happiness this time.

Cool out, his inner voice warned once again.

He left the medical examiner a voicemail, then turned his attention back to his laptop, acting as if he hadn't noticed Nia ogling her phone.

"You are not gonna believe this," she said, handing him her cell. "Read that text from Ivy."

"Text from Ivy?" Drew repeated, his neck burning with shame.

And here you were, assuming she was chatting with a man...

He took the phone and scanned the message.

Hey big sis. Funny you asked about the next event at Shelby's. There's a rave happening at midnight tonight. But you DID NOT hear that from me and you'd better not tell your cohorts. If it gets shut down, everyone's gonna assume I snitched thanks to you being a cop. So keep it on the hush!

"Wow," Drew said. "You know what this means? The universe is working in our favor. Tonight is gonna generate some solid new leads. Thanks for contacting Ivy and getting that intel."

"Of course. Thanks for coming up with the idea to pass out Katie's photo at the rave. We make a good team," Nia added with a wink.

The small yet sensual gesture sent a rush of heat straight through Drew's gut that roused below his belt. Forcing his eyes toward the clock hanging above her head, he said, "It's already after twelve. Why don't we figure out tonight's game plan over lunch? Then maybe cut out early. If the rave doesn't start until midnight, we should probably try and get some rest."

"Good idea. These days, I'm never even out until midnight, let alone arriving somewhere at such an ungodly hour."

"Same here. I never had late nights like this unless it was…"

Drew's voice faded as memories of the last New Year's Eve he and his ex-fiancée spent together crashed his mind.

"Unless it was what?" Nia asked.

"Never mind." He slammed his laptop shut and shot to his feet.

"Are you okay?"

"Yep. I'm fine," he told her, despite being far from fine.

Drew wished he had it in him to justify his reaction. To explain why the conversation had turned so triggering. But now was not the time or place to discuss the tragedy surrounding his personal life.

Chapter Ten

Nia and Drew stood outside Shelby's with Katie's flyers in hand, waiting for the partygoers to arrive. They were both dressed in dark, casual clothing and baseball caps in an attempt to blend in with the crowd.

So far, only a few people had trickled inside through a kicked-in side door, carrying lighting and DJ equipment. They'd been less than helpful when the officers flashed Katie's photo, insisting they needed to get inside and set up.

"I'm just imagining all the illegal drugs that are gonna be flowing in and out of here tonight," Nia said.

"Yeah, and unfortunately, we'll have to tackle that problem another night. We're here on a different mission. I don't want anything blocking our road to the killer."

Nia took notice when a group of young men hopped out of a pickup truck. "Here we go," she said, leading with Katie's photo as she approached. "Excuse me, have any of you seen this woman here at the factory? Or anywhere in the vicinity?"

Barely looking at the picture, they muttered an almost inaudible "Nope" before pushing past her.

Spinning around in frustration, she shouted, "Hey!" and followed the men. "You didn't even look at the—"

"Hold on," Drew said, grabbing hold of her mid-confrontation. "Let them go. The night is young. There'll be plenty more people to talk to. This investigation is a marathon, not a sprint. Tonight will be no different. All it's gonna take is one solid tip to lead us in the right direction."

Her arms relaxed within his grip. *Regroup*, Nia thought, feeling less like a lead investigator and more like a newbie fresh out of the academy. She stood taller, straightening the flyers in her hand. "You're right. I'll tamp down the aggression and play it a little cooler."

"Good. But don't lose that fighting spirit of yours. It's one of the traits I admire most about you."

Reassurance permeated within her as Drew's hand slid toward the small of her back.

"I won't…" she murmured.

The candy factory stood far back from the street, with little light surrounding the area. The building's dilapidated wood exterior looked as if it might come crashing down at any given moment. Nia couldn't understand why anyone would want to step foot inside the place. But once it was no longer considered an active crime scene and the police tape was removed, the ravers, drug addicts and squatters began using it again.

"Are you warm enough?" Drew asked when a chilly breeze blew by.

Nia zipped her tan leather jacket up to her chin and hovered closer to him. "I am now."

She took a breath, staring up at the streaks of dark gray clouds scattered across the sky. Her squinting eyes couldn't make out one single star hidden within them. The grim atmosphere was as bleak as the reason they were there. Nia just hoped their efforts wouldn't be in vain.

Boom!

The pair jolted when heavy bass rumbled from inside the factory.

"Sounds like the party is getting started," Drew said.

"Judging by all the headlights rolling up to the curb, we've got some new arrivals, too."

Anticipation swelled in Nia's chest as a crowd began to gather. She held the flyers tighter, slipping one in between her fingers to quickly pass along.

Within seconds, people came rushing toward them like a tsunami, storming past so briskly that the officers hardly had a chance to say hello. They shoved Katie's photo into the partygoers' hands anyway, shouting, "Do you know her?" while praying for a response. Almost everyone blew them off, barely glancing at the picture before tossing the flyer to the ground.

At one point Nia attempted to march inside the factory. But Drew held her back, insisting she remain calm.

"Hey, keep your head," he told her. "I don't want you getting caught up inside of there. It's too many of them and not enough of us. We've just gotta stay patient. And persistent. There's still a ton of people out here. Trust me, we'll find somebody who knows something."

Shuffling her feet to shake the excess energy, Nia nodded. "Once again, you're right."

Techno music blared through the factory's shattered windows as ravers continued to pour inside. Nia's throat burned as she yelled over the blaring drum machines. No one appeared to be listening as throngs of people brushed past her as if she weren't there. Some of them even shoved the flyers back at her. Just when she considered tossing the rest of the pictures in the air and giving up, Drew called out her name.

"Over here!" he shouted after they'd briefly gotten separated. He was surrounded by three men and two women. All of them were dressed in torn black T-shirts, leggings and platform boots, with spiked hair dyed every color of the rainbow.

As Nia scanned the group, Drew said, "Three of these guys said they've seen Katie."

"Here at the candy factory?"

One of the men pointed toward the end of the street. "No. A couple of blocks over at the Green Lizard lounge."

"When was the last time you saw her there?" Drew asked.

Shrugging his scrawny shoulders, he looked to one of the women. "I don't know. Do you remember, Adina?"

"I think it was like a couple of weeks before her body was found."

"So you know about her murder?" Nia probed.

"Um, *yeah.* I think it's safe to say everybody in this town knows. And the word is spreading. This is the first rave they've thrown at Shelby's since her death." She paused, gesturing at the huge crowd. "All these people aren't from Juniper, obviously. But after DJ Onslaught dedicated tonight to Katie, everybody from all over Colorado decided to come out and pay their respects."

Leaning toward Drew, Nia whispered, "Interesting. Most of the people we've talked to claimed to have never heard of her."

A member of the group who was sporting a purple mohawk nudged Adina. "We'd better get inside before they close the doors on us."

As they backed away, Drew called out, "Hey, thanks for that info!"

"So what do you think?" Nia asked. "Should we stay out here and see who else might know something? Or head over to the Green Lizard?"

He checked his watch, then looked out at the crowd. Partygoers were getting rowdier by the minute, practically climbing over one another trying to get into the factory. "Why don't we head over to the Green Lizard before they close? Maybe someone on the staff or even some of the patrons have seen Katie there."

"It would be even sweeter if they captured her on surveillance video at some point. Then maybe we could see who she was hanging out with, talking to, leaving with…"

"Yeah, that would be nice. Let's go see what we can find out."

Drew offered Nia his arm before pushing his way through the crowd. Her body pressed against his as he led the way, protecting her from the throng of ravers.

She'd gotten so used to looking out for herself that Nia forgot what it was like having a caring, capable man by her side. Despite Drew being a colleague, he was beginning to feel like something else. Something more. And as delusional as that may have been, it felt damn good.

When they reached the car, Drew pulled out his cell phone.

"Who are you calling this late?" Nia asked.

The moment the question escaped her lips she gasped, slapping her hand over her mouth.

"Drew, I—I am so sorry. I shouldn't have asked you that. I mean…obviously you can call whomever you want whenever you want. I don't know what possessed me to be so nosy."

"It's all good," he quipped, his sexy half smile riddled with amusement. "I was actually going to check my voicemail."

"Gotcha," Nia mumbled, biting down on her loose tongue before climbing inside the car.

Please let that be the last time you make a fool of yourself…

BY THE TIME Drew pulled into Nia's driveway, it was almost 3:00 a.m.

After leaving Shelby's, they'd headed straight to the Green Lizard. The lounge was located in a part of town that Nia seldom frequented, so she wasn't familiar with the establishment. When Drew parked in front, she realized why.

The bar looked more like a rundown shack than a place of business with its wrinkled metal roof, weathered wooden planks and foggy glass-block windows.

"Last call was fifteen minutes ago!" the bartender had yelled when they walked through the dented steel door.

"We're not here to order drinks," Drew told the puny, bald-headed man. "We're here on official police business."

The second he flashed his badge, the bartender dried his crooked fingers on his filthy apron and called for the manager. She came out from the kitchen with a towel wrapped around her head, as if she'd just washed her hair.

"May I help you?" the burly woman barked, her sparse eyebrows furrowing into her deeply creased forehead.

Nia couldn't take her eyes off the colorful tattoos running up and down both her arms. Snakes slithering around bushels of flowers spread from her wrists to her shoulders. As Drew explained why they were there, the manager began eyeing Nia so suspiciously that she stepped away, pulling out her phone and snapping photos of the lounge.

The seedy establishment appeared more like a long hallway than an actual tavern. Nia walked the length of it, the soles of her boots sticking to the warped hardwood floor. While the red fluorescent lighting was dim, it wasn't dark enough to hide the cracked vinyl barstools, dingy white walls and grimy poplar tables. Even though drinks were no longer being served, there were still several people with beer bottles in hand hovering around an old laminate jukebox.

It didn't take long for the manager to warm up to Drew. He had that effect on people—especially women. Nia attributed it to his deep, calming voice, disarming charm and uncanny ability to come up with the best one-liners at just the right time. Two minutes into a conversation and strangers felt as though they'd known him for years. The fact that he was devastatingly handsome in a rugged, approachable type of way didn't hurt matters, either.

The highlight of the night occurred when the manager admitted that Katie had been a regular at the bar, then handed over surveillance footage from the last time she'd seen her there. Nia had sung Drew's praises the whole way home for prying that evidence from the prickly woman's hands.

And now, as he walked Nia to the door, she couldn't bring herself to say good-night.

"You know I can't wait until tomorrow to watch that video, right?" she said. "I am *far* too riled up for that."

"You know what's funny? Neither can I."

"Well, then, since neither of us are ready to call it a night, why don't you come inside? I've got a refrigerator full of bar food that Ivy brought home from Bullseye and an unopened bottle of Merlot."

"That sounds amazing, actually. Because I'm starving, my fridge is currently empty and I'm all out of wine."

"Oh, wow. Yeah, you needed this invitation for more reasons than one," Nia joked before leading Drew inside.

All the lights were out, which meant Ivy wasn't home. Nia switched on a couple of lamps before tossing her things onto the console table.

As she sauntered through the living room, Drew followed closely behind. Nia could feel his eyes roaming her body. The sensation sent a shiver straight to her core.

"Should I pour the wine while you prep the food?" he asked, stopping near the couch while unzipping his camo jacket.

"No, I've got it covered. Why don't you relax. Have a seat. Watch some television while I get everything together."

The suggestion hadn't come from a place of hospitality. Nia didn't trust herself to move about the kitchen with Drew in such close proximity. It was late. She tended to make rash decisions during the wee hours of the morning—especially when it came to her libido.

"Thanks for the kind offer," he told her, "but I'd rather help you instead. That way we can get to the surveillance footage faster, and if you're up for it, maybe watch a movie afterwards."

The suggestion hung in the air like a delectable offering, waiting to be devoured.

"I'd like that," Nia replied with no hesitation.

She hovered near the fireplace as Drew pulled off his coat. She wished he hadn't worn a fitted black T-shirt as it set off his broad chest and bulging biceps.

"I—I, uh…" she stammered, pointing toward the kitchen. "I'm gonna go heat up the food."

"I'm right behind you."

Drew was slow to follow as he eyed the colorful abstract paintings hanging from the walls and black-and-white photos lining the mantel. "I love your place. And this kitchen… Is it newly renovated?"

"It is. I needed a fresh new look. So I switched out the white appliances for stainless steel and replaced the dark wood cabinets for these cream ones. They really brighten up the room, and it all works together to give off the contemporary feel I was going for."

"I agree. Everything looks great." He ran his hand along the granite countertop, brushing up against Nia as she pulled takeout containers from the refrigerator. When her hips grazed his groin, she jumped back.

"Ooh, sorry," he said, palming her back as if to steady her. "I was trying to get to the wine glasses."

Yeah, right...

Ignoring Drew's struggle to suppress a smirk, Nia pointed above his head. "They're in the cabinet to your left."

"And the wine?"

"In the corner next to the coffeemaker."

Nia filled a platter with buffalo wings, truffle mushroom flatbread and onion rings, then placed it in the microwave.

This isn't fair, she thought, watching the food rotate. Having Drew there, inside her home, felt too good. Too right. Their conversation flowed too easily. And the attraction was too strong. This was the first time she'd met a man who seemed perfect in every way. Yet he was off-limits.

"Hey," Drew said, tapping the laptop sitting on the counter. "Can we use this to review the surveillance footage?"

"Yep. Go ahead and start it up."

Once the microwave buzzed, Nia grabbed everything and set up shop on the island.

"Are you sure you've got time for all this?" he asked.

"I do. Why?"

"Well, I've already taken up the majority of your day. *And* night. There isn't anyone special who'd expect to be here with you right now?"

He's fishing...

A long sip of wine fueled her response. "Officer Taylor, are you trying to figure out whether or not I'm seeing someone?"

Nia expected a swift denial. Instead she got a head nod followed by a crooning, "Maybe…"

A tug of silence swirled between them. She turned away and began preparing their plates, taking her time before responding. Taking her lead, Drew busied himself by inserting the USB drive into the computer. His expression was neutral, as if he wasn't pressing for a response. His bouncing knees, however, told her that he was eager for a reply.

"To answer your question, no. I'm single."

Drew's brows shot up toward the ceiling. "Really?"

"Yes. Why is that so shocking?"

"Well, I mean you're beautiful, intelligent, you crack great jokes and are passionate about the things you love. You're family-oriented, and the list goes on. Bottom line, you're everything a man would want in a woman."

His words sent Nia's heart pounding against her ribcage as she slid onto the stool next to his. While she'd sensed their attraction was mutual, she had no clue his admiration ran that deep.

"Wow," she uttered. "That, uh…that was pretty unexpected. But so nice. Thank you."

"You're welcome. I'm just stating the obvious. I can't imagine you haven't heard that from a man before."

"I have. In bits and pieces from different men. It's just surprising coming from you. I didn't think you paid attention to those types of things since all we seem to talk about is the investigation or departmental policies or—"

"Anything that isn't personal?" Drew interjected.

"Yes, exactly."

"You're right. In case you hadn't noticed, it takes me a minute to warm up to people. It isn't easy letting my guard down. Especially when it comes to situations like ours. We were partnered up during a pretty tough time. But now that

I've gotten to know you, I've come to realize that you're pretty damn amazing, Nia."

Those words sent her swooning so hard that she almost fell from the stool. Propping her hand underneath her chin, she replied, "Well, I could easily say the same for you. Getting to know you has been a pleasant surprise. Not what I'd expected after the way things went down at that mentorship meeting. Let's just say I'm glad I was wrong about you."

"Thank God I was able to redeem myself," Drew joked before quickly turning serious. "So why aren't you seeing anyone?"

Nia bit into a slice of flatbread, chewing slowly while contemplating her response. "I guess the short answer is I refuse to settle."

"And what would settling look like for you?"

"Getting involved with a man who doesn't want to commit. Who isn't kind and respectful and doesn't work hard. I actually keep a mental checklist of must-haves. And if I can't tick them all off, then I pass. My friends think I'm asking for too much and should reassess my criteria. But I refuse to."

"As you should. Nothing you're asking for is unreasonable." Drew picked up his glass and leaned into her, his touch igniting sparks between them both. "Here's to you finding everything you want and deserve in a partner."

You're everything I want in a partner, Nia almost blurted. Her gaze drifted from his inviting eyes to his soft lips. They parted slightly, leaving her questioning how they'd feel pressed against hers. How he'd feel inside of her...

Shifting in her seat, she asked, "What about you? Are you seeing anyone?"

"Nope. I'm single."

"Hmm, that's not what I expected to hear."

"Yeah, well, my dating life isn't something I normally talk about."

When Drew's lips twisted into a tight expression, Nia hesitated, waiting for him to elaborate. But he didn't, instead draining his glass, then refilling it.

"You don't have to talk about it if you don't want to," she told him.

"I know. But I probably should. Holding it in hasn't been the healthiest way to cope." He picked at the cheese oozing from a mozzarella stick before proceeding. "I was engaged once. To a police detective from Aurora named Ellody. She'd moved to Juniper to be with me and was commuting back and forth while figuring out what she wanted to do with her career. But we soon realized that the distance was what made us work. Once she came here permanently, problems arose that left me questioning whether or not we were even compatible."

"What type of problems were you having?" Nia probed, unable to contain her curiosity.

"Well, when it came to finances, for instance, she was more of a spender while I'm more of a saver. I'm a neat freak, and she didn't mind a lot of clutter. She enjoyed nights out while I'm more of a homebody. Things like that. It got to the point where our differences began to outweigh the good between us. After admitting to that, we decided it would be best to end the relationship."

"Hmm, that couldn't have been easy. Especially when you two were planning on getting married."

"No, it wasn't, but..." Staring down at his steepled hands, Drew uttered, "That's not where the story ends. A few months after Ellody moved back to Aurora, we reconnected. I think we both realized we'd be better off as friends. Just as we began building a platonic relationship, she was killed in the line of duty."

"My God, Drew. I am so sorry. I had no idea…"

"Thanks. Like I said, it's something I rarely talk about. Since then, I haven't really dated. That experience was so devastating that I've pretty much closed myself off to the whole relationship thing." After a long pause, he tapped his hand against the island, then pulled the laptop closer. "But anyway, enough about me. Let's get back to business."

As Drew clicked on the portable drive, Nia pushed her plate to the side, her appetite transforming into a slight bout of nausea. Hearing the news of his ex was tragic. And while she was sympathetic toward his loss, the consequence was duly noted—Drew was not ready to love again.

"Okay, here we go," he said when an image of the Green Lizard's interior appeared on the screen.

The bar was packed. Every stool was occupied. There were rows of people standing behind them, vying for the bartender's attention. The tables were full. Groups of people with drinks in their hands were bouncing to the music.

Peering at the screen, Drew nibbled on a buffalo wing. "Any sign of Katie yet?"

"Not yet. But I'm looking."

Ten minutes into the video, Nia tapped the screen. "I think that's her. The woman in the red sweater and skinny jeans. Isn't that Katie?"

The pair watched as she approached the bar, then turned and faced the crowd.

"Oh, yeah," Drew said. "That's definitely her. Let's see who she's there with."

A group of women approached Katie, embracing her before starting up an animated conversation. As they spoke, two men walked over. One of them was wearing a baseball cap. Nia couldn't make out his face, but he appeared tall and athletic, with wide shoulders and a narrow waist. He hugged Katie tightly, then held her in his arms while whispering in her ear. The twosome began swaying back and forth. Another couple of minutes passed before his friend and the group of women drifted off, leaving Katie and the man alone.

"It's interesting how this guy has his cap pulled down so low," Nia said. "Like he doesn't want anyone to recognize him."

"Yeah, it is. Notice how he's keeping his head down, too. As if he's aware of the surveillance cameras and is trying to avoid them."

"Right. And he's staying glued to Katie's side."

The officers leaned in closer as the man began pulling her by the waist.

"Wait, what is he doing?" Drew asked.

"It looks like he's trying to drag her out of the bar."

The sight of Katie reaching for her friends was unsettling, even though she didn't appear to be under duress.

"This is so eerie," Nia said. "Here Katie's laughing and joking and having a great time. Little did she know she'd be murdered in a matter of days."

Just when it appeared as though Katie and the man were moving toward the exit, the screen flickered, then blacked out.

"Wait," Nia muttered, "What just happened?"

"I don't know."

Drew pounded the Enter and Escape keys. Both officers jolted when a new video popped up. The bar's parking lot came into view. Within minutes, Katie and her companion came back into frame.

"All right," Drew said, "we've got action again. Now let's just hope we can get a look at the guy's face this time."

The officers watched as Katie approached a large black SUV. The man opened the passenger door for her, then stared down at the ground while walking around to the driver's side.

"Come on," Nia said, both officers leaning in so close that their noses almost touched the screen. "Please look up. Show us your face..."

Suddenly, rain began to pour. The man in the video hesitated, looking up at the sky.

Air caught in Nia's throat as she struggled to process the image on the screen. But as a flash of lightning illuminated the video, there was no mistaking the man's identity.

It was Officer Davis.

Chapter Eleven

Drew pulled into his garage and headed inside the house. Tossing his messenger bag onto the kitchen table, he headed straight for the refrigerator. The half-empty bottle of wine he'd uncorked a few days ago was still sitting in the door. He resisted the urge to grab it and down the remaining malbec.

Just as he reached for a can of sparkling water his cell phone buzzed. A throbbing pain hit his left temple at the sight of Chief Mitchell's name.

"Please, no bad news," Drew mumbled before picking up. "Chief Mitchell. What's going on, sir?"

"Officer Taylor, listen. I just got back into town from my brother-in-law's funeral and wanted to follow up on the Officer Davis situation. Did you and Brooks get a chance to question him about that Katie Douglas surveillance footage?"

"We did, after he finally showed back up to work today. I'm curious about that sudden leave of absence he took."

"I think someone tipped him off about the video, so he knew you were coming for him. What did he have to say for himself?"

"First I asked why he hadn't told us that he knew Katie. He claimed he didn't think it was important enough to mention."

"Oh, come on," the chief grunted. "I don't believe that for one minute. Davis is a veteran officer, for God's sake. He knows information like that is important."

"That's exactly what I told him. After questioning him for almost thirty minutes, he finally admitted to why he hadn't come clean. He thought being connected to a murder victim would be a bad look for the force. Plus he's in a long-term relationship. So he had no business being out with Katie in the first place and didn't want his girlfriend to find out."

"What an idiot," Chief Mitchell bemoaned. "Okay, then. So are we ruling him out as a person of interest?"

"Yes, we are. No one in the department knows this except for Officer Brooks, but I had one of the crime lab technicians compare Davis's fingerprints to the evidence found at the crime scenes. They weren't a match."

"Good to know. And of course that'll stay between us. So what do you and Brooks have planned next? Do the three of us need to sit down and discuss a new course of action?"

Drew set the can of sparkling water back inside the refrigerator and pulled out a bottle of beer. The conversation was going to require something stronger than LaCroix.

"She and I have put together a game plan. We've been spending a lot of time studying the case file trying to figure out what type of person our suspect is. His character traits. What drives his behaviors. Things like that."

"And how exactly are you two doing that?"

"We're following the FBI's method. Evaluating each crime that's been committed, analyzing the scenes, studying each victim and reviewing the police reports with a fine-tooth comb. It's obvious the homicides are linked since the DNA evidence matched up. Plus those ominous clues that are being left with the victims."

"Speaking of which, I'm surprised nothing came of the wedding invitation left at Latimer Park. The nuptial already took place at the country club without incident."

"Yeah, I was shocked by that, too." Drew reached inside his bag and pulled out Violet Shields's autopsy reports. "There's gotta be something we're overlooking. Officer Brooks and I have been over the evidence hundreds of times, yet we haven't come up with any new leads."

"Keep digging, Taylor. I have faith that you two will get this case solved. In the meantime, if you need me, you know where to find me."

"Thanks, Chief." Drew's cell phone pinged against his ear. "This is Officer Brooks calling on the other line now. We'll check with you tomorrow."

He tapped the Swap button. "Hey, what's up, Nia. Chief Mitchell and I were just talking about—"

"Drew," she panted. "I need you to come to my house. Something is wrong here."

Vaulting from the chair and grabbing his keys, he headed straight for the door. "What's going on?"

"I just got home, and while I was walking up the driveway, I heard some weird, creepy ringing coming from the back of the house. So I walked around to the backyard and saw that all of my deck furniture had been rearranged. And there were two sets of wind chimes hanging from the lamp posts."

"Have you talked to Ivy? Maybe she hung them—"

"No," Nia interrupted. "It wasn't Ivy. I already talked to her and she hasn't touched a thing. And she knows I hate wind chimes, so she never would've put them up. But that's not all. Someone wrote the words *back off, bitch* in red paint across my patio table."

"I'm on my way there now. Are you still outside on the deck?"

"I am. I'm looking around trying to see if any more damage has been done."

"Do you have your gun?"

"Of course. It's right in my hand, locked and loaded."

"Listen to me, Nia. We're dealing with a deranged killer here. I don't want you roaming around out there alone without any backup. Go inside the house, lock up and wait for me to get there. I won't be long."

DREW PULLED INTO Nia's driveway and parked at the bottom near the gate. He climbed out and drew his gun, scaling the fence before entering the backyard.

The lush green lawn didn't appear to be touched. Neither did the pink butterfly bushes and green holly shrubs. But the cream-cushioned wicker loveseat, chairs and ottoman were all sitting in a straight line along the aluminum railing. Drew remembered Nia having each piece surrounding the stone firepit.

An eerie clanging rang out. His head swiveled toward the bronze tiki torch poles. Two sets of shiny blue wind chimes swung from the canisters, creating a deep, sonorous tone that sent a chill straight through him.

After pulling on latex gloves, Drew removed the bells and placed them inside a paper bag, then sent Nia a text letting her know he was there. Within seconds, the back door swung open and she came charging out.

"Thank God you're here," she moaned, running straight into his arms.

Drew's embrace tightened as she trembled against his chest. "Are you all right?"

"Not really." Nia pointed toward the house. "Somebody tore down the security camera I had mounted over the door."

With an arm securely wrapped around her waist, he led her to the doorway and studied the steel base hanging off the brick exterior. "Have you had a chance to look at the surveillance footage yet?"

"No. I wanted to wait until you got here so we could watch it together." Her head fell against his shoulder. "And that isn't all…"

"What else is going on?"

Without responding, Nia grabbed Drew's hand and led him inside the house. There, sitting on the kitchen counter, was a gift.

"What is that?" he asked.

"A present, I guess. Someone left it on my back doorstep."

Drew stepped cautiously toward the small box, eyeing its elegant silver wrapping and cream satin bow.

"I was afraid to open it," she continued. "It could be a bomb or some sort of poison, like abrin or anthrax."

"Something's telling me this isn't that type of thing. My guess is that it's another clue."

Nia backed away from the counter while shaking her head. "I don't know, Drew. I think we should contact the Postal Inspectors. They've got the specialized screening equipment needed to handle this sort of thing."

"I don't think I can wait that long. I wanna know what's in the box now." He pulled an N95 respirator mask from his bag and covered his face. "Stand back."

She hovered in the doorway while he unwrapped the box and peeled open shimmery tissue paper, revealing some sort of lacy white material.

"I can't just stand here and watch this," Nia declared, re-entering the kitchen. "Hand me a pair of gloves and mask."

Drew waited for her to slip on the protective gear before removing the lacy object and holding it in the air.

"Is that...a garter?" she asked.

"Looks like it. Why in the hell would someone leave this on your doorstep?"

"I have no idea."

Several moments passed before Nia finally spoke up, her thin tone tinged with trepidation. "I hope this doesn't have anything to do with one of my exes. I've got a couple who were bitter as hell when I broke things off. When I followed my dream of becoming a police officer, that really set the last one off."

"Would either of these exes happen to know that you hate wind chimes?"

"Oh, absolutely. At some point, one in particular tossed around the idea of us getting married, too, which I immediately shot down."

"Hence him leaving a garter belt at your doorstep, alluding to you missing out on being his bride? If he's keeping up with the news, then he'd know you're one of the lead investigators on the case. He could've done this as a way to throw you off your game."

"Yep. And he was petty as hell, too. So I would not put something like this past him."

Nia cringed at the thought as she reached inside a drawer and pulled out a plastic baggie. After snapping several photos of the garter, Drew slipped it inside the bag along with the gift box and wrapping paper.

"I'll get this to the crime lab first thing in the morning. See if it matches up with anyone in CODIS."

"And in the meantime, I should go through my last ex's

garbage to try and find a disposable cup, a straw…anything that would contain his DNA."

"Um, let's wait on the results from the lab before you go doing all that. You never know. This time we just might get a hit. For now, why don't we check out the surveillance footage from the backyard?"

"I'll pull it up."

As Nia launched the video, Drew thought about Ivy. "Hey, you mentioned that your sister has been staying with a friend from work, right?"

"I did. It's just easier that way since she doesn't have a car. She and her friend Madison set their schedules so that they'd cover the same shifts. It's such a relief, because knowing Ivy, she'd be on public transportation or hitching rides with strangers at all hours of the night."

Drew glanced at the back door, reminded of the security camera that had been stolen. "Yeah, that is a relief. For her at least. But what about you? I could put a cop car on the block to keep an eye on your house. I'd feel much better if you weren't here alone though. Is there anywhere else you could stay for the time being? Your parents' house? Or Madison's? At least until we get a suspect in custody."

"Uh, *no.* Madison has at least two other women who work at Bullseye living with her, and that isn't counting Ivy. As for my parents, they've got my uncle Jeffrey staying with them, plus they've somehow managed to hoard every piece of furniture they have ever purchased in life inside that house. So there's no room for me. But don't worry. I'll be fine right here in my own home, with my doors locked, security system on and Glock fully loaded."

When Drew studied Nia's strained expression, he could sense the tension behind her narrowing eyes as they peered at the computer screen. Rather than stress her out further, he took the hint and dropped the subject.

"The surveillance footage is up and running," she said, turning the laptop in his direction. "It was recorded this morning. I left for work at about seven forty-five, so the suspect got here sometime after that. I'll speed up the video until we see some movement."

Several minutes passed before Drew nudged her hand. "Hold on. Go back a few seconds. I think I just saw something."

"Okay. I'll slow it down, too. I think I may have seen a shadow come into view, but I'm not sure…"

The thirty-seven minute mark flashed on the screen when Nia began replaying the tape. Just as she set the view percentage to 150, someone jumped the fence near the driveway, then hid behind the side of the house.

"Did you see that?" Drew asked.

"I did. Let me rewind it again."

After playing the footage back once more, he realized the perp was moving too fast to get a good look at him. He appeared to be wearing a red flannel shirt, black cargo pants and Timberland boots. His head was covered with a red baseball cap, and his face was hidden behind a black mask.

"I'm trying to see what this man looks like," Nia said, rewinding and replaying the footage again, "but he's covered from head to toe. From what I can tell, he looks tall. And slim. Unlike my ex."

"His silhouette is actually similar to the suspect who knocked the camera off the front of your house."

"It sure is. So we're probably dealing with the same person here."

A few seconds later, the film showed the security camera beginning to shake.

"Will you look at this," Nia lamented. "This guy is using the same tactic he did when he stole the other camera."

"And he made sure to knock it down before rearranging the furniture, hanging the wind chimes and leaving the garter. I'll give it to him. The man is going to great lengths to remain unrecognizable."

When Nia dropped her head in her hands, Drew placed an arm around her.

"I'm so sorry," he murmured. "We're gonna catch this guy. That much I can promise you."

"Yeah, but how? And why the sudden attack on me? Is it because I'm connected to the investigation, or is this something more? Something deeper?"

Drew bit his jaw as he stared at the black-and-white static flickering across the screen. "Unfortunately, I don't have the answers to those questions. *Yet.* But I will. Because one thing I don't do is make promises I can't keep."

She nodded, muttering into her hands, "This is such a mess. Did you see the article on the front page of *The Juniper Herald* this morning?"

"I did. And I noticed a few of the guys around the station reading it, then slamming their laptops shut when they saw me. That headline was scathing, too. 'Juniper PD Doesn't Have What It Takes to Catch a Killer.'"

"Yeah, that really pissed me off. More support and less criticism would go a long way here." Nia hesitated, staring at Drew through damp eyes. "But...*do* we have what it takes?"

"Of course we do. You know our motto. This is a marathon. Not a sprint. Like Chief Mitchell once told me, working in the field of criminal justice means playing the long game. And if we work hard enough, we'll get this case solved."

Straightening her back against the stool, Nia replied, "You're right. So where do we go from here? Back to the criminal profile we've been building?"

"I think that would be our best bet. I was just telling the chief that once we have a good understanding of who we're dealing with, we'll have a better chance of apprehending him."

"I'll pull that document up now," she said right before her cell phone pinged.

Drew watched as her tense expression softened, the light suddenly returning to her deep brown eyes. Resisting the urge to peer down at her phone, he said, "Good news?"

"Yeah, that was Ivy. Since we've got this maniac roaming the streets, I've asked her to check in with me a couple times a day, just to let me know she's okay. Surprisingly it's working. She just got to Bullseye and is covering somebody else's shift, so she'll be there until late tonight. She's gonna let me know once she's off and back at Madison's."

"I like that you're keeping up with her."

Or are you relieved to hear that she wasn't communicating with a man?

Ignoring the irritating thought, Drew asked, "Does Ivy know what's been going on here at the house?"

"She does. Which is why she rarely comes back here now. But I told her that whenever she needs to drop in to make sure I'm home first."

Drew's gut urged him to reiterate that it would be good if Nia found somewhere else to stay. At least for the near future. But he refrained. After she'd made it clear that she wanted to remain in her house, he knew he couldn't force her.

"So let's talk about this criminal profile we're building," Nia said. "So far, we've deduced that our suspect is between the ages of thirty-eight and forty-five. He's about six feet tall, maybe a little taller, and no more than a hundred-and-eighty pounds. He is intelligent and well educated, with at least a bachelor's degree. We think he's extroverted and charismatic, and meeting these women in social or public settings, like bars, clubs and gyms. He's familiar with Juniper but probably doesn't live here, and he's definitely killed before."

"Right." Drew swiped open the Notes app on his phone and tapped the bulleted list of profile traits. "He's methodical. Very careful in his planning. Which has a lot to do with why he has yet to be caught. Our suspect is mission-oriented in that he's going after young women and killing them in the same manner. He also enjoys the control he has over the victims once he gets them alone."

"And since the women's toxicology reports came back negative, we know they were fully aware of what was happening to them during their attacks. It's as if the suspect doesn't want them to be sedated because he gets off on their fear."

The clicking of Nia's laptop keys suddenly stopped. She moaned loudly, leaning to one side while clutching her hip.

"Are you okay?" Drew asked.

"I am. I think it's these stools. The sleek Italian lacquer look seemed like a good idea when I was remodeling the kitchen. But they're not the most comfortable pieces of furniture I own." She glanced over at the clock on the microwave. "I'll tell you what. It's dinnertime, and I haven't eaten yet. Have you?"

"No. You called right after I got home from the station. I ran over here so fast that I didn't get a chance to even think about food. But now that you mention it, I'm starving."

Grasping the metal sides of her seat, Nia slowly stood.

"Why don't we take this into the living room where we can stretch out on the couch, and I'll order takeout?"

Drew's lips parted. But he failed to respond while watching her dip to one side and knead her gluteal muscles. The move accentuated every curve in her fitted navy slacks, leading to thoughts of those long, lithe legs wrapped around his waist.

"So what do you think?" she asked, looking up at him.

Quickly turning away, he said, "That sounds good," while hoping she hadn't noticed him gawking. "We could do Thai or Mexican…"

"Ooh, yes. Mexican would be perfect." She grabbed her phone and began typing away. "I'll order from Zapata Cove since we both love that place. Can you grab a bottle of cabernet sauvignon from the fridge? Then we'll head to the living room and get back to work."

"You got it."

Drew collected the wine and glasses, then followed Nia out of the kitchen. On the way past the island, he caught a glimpse of the evidence bags. They were a stark reminder of the imminent danger surrounding her home.

His grip on the bottle tightened. Somehow, he had to convince her that she could no longer stay there alone.

Chapter Twelve

Nia tapped her fingernails against her glass and glanced around The Sphinx Hotel's bar once again. There was still no sign of Shane Anderson.

She pulled her cell phone from her snakeskin clutch and opened the Someone for Everyone app. After scrolling through the messages, she tapped on the last one he'd sent her.

Hello beautiful. I'm so glad you're available this weekend. Can't wait to meet you. I'll see you Saturday night at 7:00 p.m. inside the Sphinx's Solar Lounge bar. Looking forward to it. xx, S

Nia closed out of the app, then immediately reopened it, deciding to send Shane a message in case he'd forgotten about their date.

Hi there. I'm at The Sphinx, sitting at the bar inside the lounge. Hope everything is okay and you're still able to make it. xx, N

She checked the time. It was 7:41 p.m. She'd give him ten more minutes. If he hadn't arrived by then, she would leave.

"Another pinot grigio, ma'am?" the bartender asked.

"No, I'm fine for now. Thank you."

Nia gripped the stem between her fingertips and twirled the glass along the mahogany bar's shiny surface. The uncertainty bubbling inside her chest had exploded into pangs of anxiety. She'd been looking forward to this evening all week. Thanks to the investigation, she couldn't remember the last time she'd been out socially. As for an actual date, it had been months.

Nia needed this night. Her entire life had begun to center around work. There was no reprieve. The majority of her days were filled with frustration considering the case had hit a wall. No amount of evidence analysis, criminal profiling, interrogating or surveilling had delivered any answers. The clues she and Drew had gathered revealed no new leads. And the DNA left at the crime scenes, which they continuously ran through CODIS, had yet to identify a suspect.

But the investigation wasn't Nia's only concern. There was also Drew. The more time the pair spent together, the deeper her attraction grew. It was getting to the point where she couldn't be around him without blushing underneath his piercing gaze or tingling at the slightest touch of his hand. His presence was beginning to drive her crazy. Yet there was no getting away from him. They had a killer to apprehend. So in the meantime she needed a distraction, and Nia was hoping it would be Shane.

After pulling the neckline of her cream sweater dress over her plunging cleavage, Nia took another look around the bar. This was the first time she'd been there since the hotel had been renovated. The lounge was sleek, with its midnight blue walls, warm crystal pendant lighting and contemporary pewter furniture. The seductive ambience set the perfect mood for a date. But from the look of things, it appeared as if Nia would be going solo.

Other than a few couples scattered about and a rowdy bridal party, the place was fairly empty. She checked the entrance. Still no tall, dapper man dressed in a suit walking through the door to meet her.

Just as she drained her glass, Nia's phone pinged. She almost choked on the last swallow of wine trying to check the notification. Hoping to see Shane's name, she swiped open the screen. Disappointment pushed her back against the chair at the sight of Ivy's message.

Hey! Just letting you know I'm working another double shift tonight then going out afterwards. If you don't hear from me again, it's because I'll be passed out on Madison's couch. Luv you!

For a brief moment, Nia considered stopping by the Bullseye and hanging out with Ivy for a bit. She hated the idea of having gone through over two hours of preparation just to head back home. Somebody needed to see her new dress, wavy curls and perfectly applied makeup.

But by the time she paid for her drink and headed toward the parking lot, all Nia wanted to do was curl up on the couch with a deep-dish pizza and a gruesome horror movie to match her mood.

"I cannot *believe* this man just wasted my time," she grumbled, slamming the car door and revving the engine.

She pulled out of the lot and jetted down the street. The bottoms of her feet went numb inside her tan stiletto boots as she pressed down on the accelerator. Light reflecting off the streetlamps blurred. Lost in her thoughts, Nia was reminded of why she seldom put herself out there. The inevitable disappointment was unbearable.

But she'd grown tired of sitting around the house waiting for someone to come along. As her mother always said, the man of her dreams wasn't going to just come knocking at her door. "Don't waste the pretty," she would tell her. "Get out there and let him find you."

And I did. Just to get stood up.

Nia made a left turn on Dobel Lane, her stomach rumbling with emotion as hot tears stung her eyes. The truth of the matter was right in front of her, but she'd blocked it from her mind. This had nothing to do with Shane or being stood up or putting herself out there in hopes of finding the right man. The right man was already in her life. It was Drew. Yet there was nothing she could do about it. Because Nia still didn't feel comfortable dating a colleague, and Drew was still healing from his tragic past.

"So basically," she whispered, "stop worrying about a relationship and focus on the investigation."

The words burned as they left her lips. All practicalities aside, there was no denying that she wanted love in her life.

As she made a left turn down Mountain View Drive, Nia turned on her high beams. Streetlights on the long stretch of road were few and far between. The lack of sufficient lighting almost caused her to hit a deer last time she'd driven here.

So concentrate, she thought, willing herself to keep her eyes on the street and off the phone as she checked for a message from Shane.

The farther she drove, the more Nia felt as if she were heading down a bleak, never-ending passageway. Loneliness simmered inside her head. Despite having no one to go home to, she focused on curling up on the couch with that pizza and movie.

Just as she turned on the radio, a pair of blinding headlights lit up her car's interior. Nia peered into the rearview mirror. It looked as if someone was trying to get her attention. But then the lights flickered erratically, appearing defective.

Thinking nothing of it, she turned up the volume on a '90's R & B satellite station, bobbing her head as Mary J. Blige's "Real Love" piped through the speakers.

"I'm searching for a real looove," Nia sang. "Someone to set my heart free…"

She stopped abruptly, realizing the lyrics were doing nothing to lighten her mood. Neither did another glance at her phone as there were still no new notifications.

Nia contemplated calling Drew under the guise of discussing the investigation. But she really just wanted to hear his voice. A witty Drew-ism or inside joke would undoubtedly lift her spirits.

The screech of spinning tires squealed behind her. Whipping her head toward the side-view mirror, Nia noticed the car with the flickering lights tailing her.

"What in the hell are you doing?"

She shifted her focus back to the dark road in front of her. Craning her neck, she hoped the intersection would come into view. It didn't. She still had a ways to go.

Nia pressed down on the accelerator. Maybe if she sped up the tailgater would back off. He didn't.

An unnerving sense of panic took hold of Nia's joints. Her head jerked from right to left. There was nothing but massive ponderosa pines standing guard on either side of her. She faced forward, gripping the steering wheel tighter while eyeing the pitch-black stretch of road.

Vroom!

The revving engine blared loud enough to drown out Nia's music. As the car loomed closer, she reached inside her clutch and felt around for her gun. Just having it in her lap would make her feel more secure. And if she needed it, she'd be ready to use it.

Her eyes darted from the rear- to side-view mirrors as she struggled to keep an eye on the road. "*Dammit*," she hissed, her fingers scrambling over her keys, wallet and compact. But no gun. It wasn't there.

"Where the hell did I..."

Her voice trailed off as she remembered rushing out of the house so quickly that she'd left it inside the hall closet.

A string of curses spewed from her lips as the car rode her bumper. Pounding the voice control button on the steering wheel, she yelled, "Call Drew!"

Please pick up.

On the third ring, he answered.

"Hey, Nia. I was just thinking about you. What's going on?"

Stay calm. Maybe it's nothing and you're just being paranoid.

She blew an unsteady exhale as the sound of his voice soothed her unraveling nerves. "Hey, Drew." Before she got started, Nia took another look in the rearview mirror. The car seemed to be farther away. The sight slowed her racing heartbeat to a semi-normal pace.

"Are you okay?" he asked. "You sound strange."

"I'm—I hope so. I was out at the Solar Lounge, and I'm on my way home now—"

"Wait, you were hanging out at The Sphinx Hotel?" Drew emitted a light chuckle. "Which one of your bougie girlfriends recommended that place? I heard that since the renovation, the drinks start at about thirty dollars a pop and the attire is designer only."

Normally his teasing would've summoned a laugh. But not tonight.

"Nia? You still there?"

"Yes, I'm here. Sorry. I'm on Mountain View Drive and this dark stretch of road has completely thrown me off—"

Her voice broke. Emotions swelled in her throat. Hearing Drew on the other end of the phone sent words dangling from her tongue that she had no intention of sharing.

"I've had a really rough night," she divulged.

"Why? What happened?"

His tone, thick with alarm, disarmed Nia. Tears welled as she pulled in a rush of air. "I wasn't out with my girlfriends. I was on a date. Or at least I was supposed to be. But I got stood up."

She held her breath, waiting for him to respond. The other end of the line went silent. Nia checked the phone to see if the call had dropped. Reception in the area was known to be spotty.

"Drew? Can you hear me?"

"Yes. I can hear you. So, you were out on a date?"

"I was *supposed* to be on a date. But the guy didn't show up."

"Who's the guy?"

His voice was laced with irritation, leaving Nia wishing she'd never brought it up.

Too late for that now...

"His name is Shane. Shane Anderson. He's new to Juniper."

After a long, awkward pause, Drew asked, "Where did you two meet?"

What's up with the interrogation? she almost blurted.

But instead she replied, "We connected through a dating app."

Nia winced at the sound of his repulsed sigh.

"A *dating* app? Really, Nia? So I guess you've forgotten there's a deranged killer running around town. Despite you being a police officer and all, it isn't very wise of you to be hooking up with random strangers—"

"Okay, hold on," she interjected, instantly regretting her decision to call him. "First of all, I'm not *hooking up* with anyone. This man and I have been corresponding for quite some time now, and all we were planning was to meet up for drinks. Secondly, I like to think that I'm a pretty good judge of character. He seemed nice, he's successful… Nothing about him screamed crazed murderer."

"Come on, Nia. You're smarter than that. Do you know how many murderers *seem* nice? Have families? And lead normal lives outside of killing people on the side?"

Curiosity eclipsed her annoyance as Drew rambled on. His genuine concern for her safety was obvious. But his snarky commentary seemed rooted in jealousy. Nia knew she could take care of herself. After living in Juniper her entire life, she didn't need a lecture on how to move around town—nor did she want the investigation to hinder her love life.

But Drew wasn't completely wrong in his sentiments. And she didn't want the night to put a damper on their partnership. So she relented, saying, "Look, I hear you. You're right. You can't judge a killer by his outward appearance."

"*Thank* you. And look, I'm not trying to tell you how to live your life. I'm just looking out for your safety. Because I would hate for something to happen to you—"

Bam!

Nia's forehead banged against the steering wheel. She

bounced against the back of the seat, her wide eyes unable to make out the road ahead.

Disoriented, she gripped her pounding head and blinked rapidly, struggling to clear her blurred vision.

"Nia?" Drew said.

Boom!

Her car careened toward the side of the road, skidding along the gravel before spinning out of control.

"Nia!" he yelled. "What the hell is going on?"

The vehicle that had been tailing her came flying toward the driver's door. She pounded the accelerator and jerked the steering wheel. The car missed hers by a few inches. Swiveling toward the back windshield, Nia watched as the car swerved along the shoulder.

"Drew!" Nia screamed. "Somebody hit my car. I—I'm being attacked!"

"Where are you?"

"I'm still on Mountain View Drive."

"Hold on. I'm coming to you now."

As the assailant's vehicle backed away from the shoulder, Nia slammed the accelerator into the floorboard. "Don't bother. By the time you get here, I'll be long gone."

"Listen to me, Nia. Do not go home. Go straight to the police station. Better yet, just come here. My house is closer to Mountain View. My gun and I will be waiting right out front. I'll text Officer Ryan and the other officers on duty and send them your way."

"Thank you," she choked, her fingers cramping around the steering wheel.

Nia's eyes darted toward the side-view mirror. The assailant's car was gaining speed. "I'm trying to get a look at the make and model of this vehicle. But it's so damn dark out here. I think it's some sort of black sedan."

"I'm guessing you can't see the license plate either?"

"No. Not at all."

"Don't worry about it," Drew assured her. "I'll get it when he comes my way. I'm already outside waiting. You've got your weapon in hand, right?"

She gritted her teeth, pissed at herself for leaving it behind.

"*Nia?* Are you still there?"

"I'm here. I, um… No, I don't have my gun. I was so busy rushing out of the house that I forgot to grab it."

Several moments passed before Drew spoke up.

"Don't let that happen again," he warned. "*Especially* when you're going to meet up with a stranger."

"I won't," she told him, her voice small against his commanding tone.

Nia's angst subsided briefly when the intersection appeared up ahead. But just as she reached the corner of the road, those flashing headlights glared behind her.

Trepidation hit as she contemplated what would happen if she stopped—the attacker would ram her into the four-way crossing. But driving straight through could cause an accident.

Pivoting from right to left, Nia saw no cars in the vicinity. The vehicle behind her loomed closer and didn't appear to be slowing down.

Just go!

She floored it, flying through the red light, then making a sharp left turn.

"Where are you now?" Drew asked.

"On Kennedy Boulevard." She glanced in the mirror. The assailant's car was right behind her. "And I've still got company."

"Well, just keep coming this way. Officer Ryan and the rest of the crew are en route."

Nia sat so rigidly that her back began to spasm. She leaned forward, shuddering when the other driver's engine roared. The increased speed sent clouds of smoke billowing through the air. He laid on the horn, causing her to swerve uncontrollably.

"Dammit!" she shrieked, jerking the steering wheel from side to side while struggling to regain control.

Gambel Oak Street was up ahead. She was only a couple of blocks away from Drew's house.

You're almost there…

"Talk to me," he said. "Can you still see the vehicle—"

Boom!

"He hit me again!" Nia screamed. "Where the hell is my backup?"

The sound of pounding footsteps beat through her car's speakers.

"That's it," Drew panted. "I'm coming to you. Now!"

"No, just stay where you are! I'm almost there."

The attacker's ultrabright high beams were blinding. Nia angled her rearview mirror until the lights reflected off his windshield. Within seconds, his car went spinning before coming to an abrupt halt.

"*Yes!* I think I may have…"

Nia's voice faded at the piercing screech of tires as the assailant's car skidded along the pavement.

A glance in the mirror sent her chest pounding. Her assailant was back on the road and gaining speed.

Hooking a sharp left onto Belle Lane, Nia huffed, "I'm right around the corner from your house. And I finally hear sirens. Tell the other officers to block off each end of your street so that this maniac will be surrounded."

"I'm on it."

She drove toward another intersection. The light was red.

As vehicles heading north drove through their green light, she ran hers, bobbing and weaving through traffic until reaching the other side.

"I'm on your block, Drew!" Nia said after making a right turn down Burr Ridge Avenue.

"I see you. Keep coming this way!"

Relief cooled her burning skin at the sight of him standing in the middle of the road. Cop cars hovered on either end of the street. Nia pulled in front of Drew's house and waited for the car that had been terrorizing her to appear. It didn't.

"Where is this guy?" Drew asked, his head swiveling from one end of the block to the other.

"I don't know. He was—he was just…"

Swallowing the whimper creeping up her throat, Nia climbed out, desperate to apprehend her attacker. Wobbling legs sent her stumbling against the doorframe. Drew caught her, holding on tight as Nia's body collapsed against his.

"It's okay," he assured her. "You're fine. I've got you."

She wrapped her arms around his waist and stared down the street. Officers jumped out of their cars and drew their weapons, covering every inch of the vicinity. The assailant was nowhere in sight.

"He knows," she said, her head falling against Drew's chest. "He knows I was coming to your house. So he kept going."

Drew held her close while calling Officer Ryan. "Hey, the suspect didn't follow Nia all the way here. I need for you all to get back out there and find him."

As he continued giving the officer instructions, Nia closed her eyes. An incoming migraine throbbed over her right eye. The roar of an engine sent her shaking in Drew's embrace. But it was Juniper PD, speeding off in search of the assailant.

"Wow," Drew uttered. "That bastard really did a number on your car."

Nia's eyes shot open. The left side of her bumper was completely hanging off while the trunk had been rammed into the backseat.

The terror that had been pulsating through her joints ignited a fiery anger.

"Drew, it's time to come up with a new game plan."

"It most certainly is. And we will. For now, I'll have forensics analyze your car while we do everything in our power to hunt down your attacker."

Too exhausted to respond, Nia reached inside the car and grabbed her cell phone.

"What are you doing?" Drew asked.

"Calling an Uber. I've been enough of an imposition. I just wanna go home, crawl into bed and—"

"Nia," he interrupted, "are you being serious right now? First of all, you're far from an imposition. You are my partner. It's my duty to be here for you. Secondly, I don't think you need to go home. You shouldn't be alone right now. Why don't you stay here with me?"

The suggestion eased Nia's bruised emotions. The offer to stay was touching. And tempting. Despite her desire to show strength in the moment, she softened underneath the weight of Drew's concern.

"I'd like that," she whispered. "Thank you."

"Of course. And just so you know, that invitation is open-ended. You can stay here for as long as you want."

With his arm securely wrapped around her, Drew led Nia up the walkway. Her head, no longer throbbing, fell against his shoulder as her mind churned in a hundred different directions.

She thought about Shane standing her up and the violent car chase that followed. Were the two incidents related? And did they somehow link back to the investigation?

"Come on in," Drew said, opening the door and leading her inside. "Make yourself at home. Anything you want or need, just say the word."

The sight of his softly lit living room came into view. The crackling fireplace cast a warm glow over the space. Cream throw pillows lined a chocolate brown leather sofa. Linen drapes hung from the windows. A game of chess sat in the middle of a plush coffee table ottoman. The faint scent of espresso lingered in the air.

Nia exhaled, the tension in her body slowly dissipating.

"You all right?" he murmured, his lips so close to her ear that his breath teased her lobe.

"Not yet. But I will be."

Chapter Thirteen

Drew trudged out of Chief Mitchell's office and returned to his desk, collapsing into his chair. His boss had requested an impromptu update on the case, and it killed him that he had nothing new to report.

It had been almost two weeks since Nia's attack. Police were unsuccessful in tracking down her assailant. With no new leads on the serial killer investigation, the chief was getting frustrated. The amount of pressure that the media and community were putting on the department was becoming unbearable. Chief Mitchell had even asked Drew whether he thought it would be a good idea to let one of the more seasoned homicide detectives take over the case.

"Absolutely not," Drew told him. "Officer Brooks and I are keeping the homicide team up-to-date and welcoming their input. However, we've put a lot of work into this investigation and the momentum is building. Trust me, we're getting closer."

His vow seemed to work as the chief ended the meeting without bumping his lead officer status. But even Drew was getting tired of hearing himself make promises that he had yet to keep.

It's time for some action…

The unsolved case wasn't the only thing bothering him.

It had been almost a week since Nia returned home. After days of keeping watch on her house, Officer Ryan saw no signs of suspicious activity. So she felt comfortable enough to go back. Drew, on the other hand, did not—especially now that Ivy was seldom there anymore. He'd expressed that to Nia, even adding that she was more than welcome to keep staying with him. But she'd refused, while promising to remain on high alert at all times.

Drew sensed that Nia felt she'd become a burden staying at his place. What she didn't realize was that her presence filled his home with a comfort he'd missed. Since losing his ex, that void was something he hadn't even acknowledged until Nia came along.

Working and living together had created a deeper bond between them. They'd spend time at the station piecing together evidence while continuing to build their criminal profile. At night they'd hang out at his place, avoiding talk of the investigation while preparing dinner or playing Scrabble. Their organic connection was intoxicating, to the point where Drew found himself imagining Nia being more than just a colleague.

It'd felt like a punch to the gut when she told him she needed to go back home. The news almost caused him to profess his feelings for her. But Drew held back, knowing how resistant Nia was to workplace romances. He did, however, wonder how long he could keep this up. Because at some point he'd have to face a hard truth—he had completely fallen for her.

Drew took a sip of his lukewarm coffee and focused on the computer screen. Katie Douglas's Instagram feed was still on display. He'd been scrolling through it before being called into the chief's office, hoping to get a better understanding of her lifestyle. He studied each post, scrutinizing the captions along with the locations and people she'd tagged.

One thing was for sure—if anybody was looking for Katie, all they'd have to do was turn to her social media to find her. By the time he'd gotten to the third post, Drew knew that she'd worked as a marketing coordinator at Next Level Productions. Her Friday nights were spent at The Golden Standard for happy hour. Every other Saturday, Katie and her sister had gone for manicures and pedicures at Betty's Day Spa. A little further in and he learned she'd been a regular at the candy factory's raves.

As Drew searched for photos taken at the Green Lizard lounge, he realized there were none. There also wasn't any evidence that she'd hung out with Officer Davis. Drew assumed the pair had some sort of understanding since he was in a relationship.

Things had been icy between him and Officer Davis since news of the fling surfaced. Drew couldn't get past the fact that Davis hadn't come clean in the beginning. He could've seen something that may have assisted in the case. In Drew's eyes, any officer willing to put his own personal interest over a murder investigation didn't deserve to be on the force.

A loud clamor and string of "Good mornings" pulled Drew from his thought. He peeked over the top of his cubicle wall, watching as Nia sauntered toward the break room. His eyes weren't the only ones following the officer as several heads turned in her direction.

"Ugh," he grumbled at the sight of their ogling expressions.

The buzz of an incoming text message from Tim served as a welcome distraction.

Taylor! Hope all is well, man. Just checking in with a quick update. I'm doing at-home physical therapy sessions three days a week now. So improvements are happening. Hoping to be back on the force soon. How are things going with the investigation? Any updates on the jerk that hit me?

Drew swallowed down the sizzle of defeat burning his throat. Not only was the investigation at a standstill, but they had yet to find the driver who'd hit Tim.

Just as he began composing a response, footsteps sounded near his desk.

"Drew!"

He spun around and saw Nia standing over him, a thin sheet of perspiration covering her face.

She shoved her cell phone into his hand. "Look at this!"

Peering at the screen, he homed in on a photo of her sitting at a bar. She was all done up, wearing a beautiful cream dress and sipping a glass of wine.

"Hmph," Drew grunted before handing her the phone back. "You ran over here in a panic just so I could tell you how good you look in that picture?"

"*No*," she hissed, jamming her fingertip against the screen. "Read the text underneath it."

"The what?" He leaned in and eyed the message.

How gorgeous were you on this night?? Too bad you got stood up. Better luck next time. And another thing. Keep hunting for the Juniper serial killer and watch the bodies pile up...

"Wait—someone just sent this to you?"

"Yes," Nia confirmed, pulling up a chair. "From an anonymous number. This photo was taken the night I went to

The Sphinx Hotel to meet up with that guy from the dating app. I'm convinced he's behind this. Behind *all* of this."

"All of this, meaning…"

"The security cameras being knocked off my house. The wedding invitation, garter and wind chimes. The re-arranged deck furniture. The car chase. And maybe even the murders. Keep in mind we connected through the same dating app that was found on Katie's phone. If we get ahold of Violet's cell and find out she was using the app, too, then I think that'll pretty much confirm my suspicions."

"Speaking of that dating app, I need to follow up with Officer Ryan on the subpoena situation. Did you ever hear back from the administrator?"

"No, I didn't." Nia opened Someone for Everyone on her phone. "But you know what's interesting? The day after Shane stood me up, he completely disappeared off the app. His profile is gone and so are all of his photos and the messages we exchanged."

"Yeah, that's very interesting. And telling." Drew paused when he heard Officer Ryan's voice nearby. "Hey, Ryan! What's the latest on the subpoena we sent to that dating app?"

"The administrator objected to it. So I filed a motion to compel. Now I'm just waiting to hear back from the court."

"All right. Keep me posted."

Drew emitted a frustrated groan before draining his cup. "I need more coffee. And some answers regarding this damn investigation."

As Nia stared at his computer screen, he turned it toward her.

"I've been going through Katie's social media trying to figure out her patterns. See where she'd been going. Who she'd hung out with."

"I've been doing the same thing with Violet. And I'm noticing that their Instagram feeds are practically identical. Same aesthetic, same amount of oversharing. Both of their lives were like an open book."

"And that's a dangerous way to live these days. Which is why I mostly avoid social media. The couple of accounts that I do have are set to private."

A knock against Drew's cubicle sent both officers spinning in their chairs.

"Hey, Officer Mills," Drew said. "What's up?"

"I heard you two over here discussing the investigation. Did you get my email?"

"No, I didn't. When did you send it?"

"Early this morning. You know how you'd been waiting on Violet Shields's family to locate her cell phone?"

"I do."

"Well, I reached out to them and got the name of her carrier, then put in a request for the data. The company's working on gathering it now."

"What about a warrant?" Nia asked. "Won't they need that before releasing the information?"

"They will, which is why I put in an urgent request for one this morning. I should receive it later today. Once I turn that over, the carrier said they'd send the data ASAP."

"Mills." Drew gave the officer an enthusiastic high five. "My man. Thank you for doing that."

"Of course. Teamwork makes the dream work. Isn't that what Chief Mitchell always says?"

"Indeed it is. Oh, and speaking of teamwork, could you be sure to include Officer Brooks on any correspondence you send to me? Since we're partners on this case, whatever I need to see, she'll need to see as well."

Officer Mills glanced down at Nia, his grin fading into a

sheepish expression. "Sure thing, Taylor. Sorry about that, Officer Brooks. I'll head back to my desk and forward everything to you now."

"Thanks. I'd appreciate it."

Nia gave Drew a look as the officer shuffled off. "I guess some of these guys still see me as the rookie cop, standing on the sidelines while you do all the work."

"Just give them some time to get used to things. I'm sure once Tim was unable to work the investigation with me, several of these guys thought they'd get his spot. So there might be a little envy happening here, too. But don't sweat it. They'll get over it. Especially after you and I solve this case."

"And even if they don't, I'm grateful that you have my back. On a positive note, I see why you pushed so hard for Chief Mitchell to hire a tech expert earlier this year. Between Katie's and Violet's phone data, we should definitely get some—"

"Officer Taylor!"

Drew and Nia both jumped to their feet at the alarm in Chief Mitchell's voice.

"Where the hell is Officer Taylor?" he asked, scrambling around the middle of the floor.

"I'm right here at my desk, sir. What's going on?"

The officer recoiled when Chief Mitchell turned to him, his pale expression distorted with agony. "I just got a call. There's been another murder."

"There's been a *what*?" Nia snapped. "Where? Please don't say the Charlie Sifford Country Club."

"No. It was at a residence—eight-four twenty-one Birchwood Lane. I need you two to get over there immediately. Officer Davis got the initial call over the radio and he's already en route. I'm right behind you."

"We—we're on it," Drew choked, turning to Nia.

The touch of her hand gave him a shot of reassurance.

"We got this," she said, somehow knowing that was exactly what he needed to hear.

"Thank you," he whispered before they jetted toward the exit.

Chapter Fourteen

Drew could hear the panic in Nia's voice as they sped down Stoney Drive, then turned onto Birchwood Lane.

"If we're dealing with the same killer here," she breathed, "then he's switching things up on us. Why would he suddenly go from public to private property? Especially after the last clue was all about the country club?"

"Good question. He's probably trying to catch us up. Confuse us so that his next moves won't be too obvious. Either that, or this murder has nothing to do with our investigation."

"I would hate to think that we've got *two* killers on our hands."

The instant Drew pulled in front of the victim's home, Nia hopped out of the car and lifted the trunk. Both officers slipped on their protective gear, grabbed their evidence collection kits and rushed up the walkway.

Officer Adams had already begun cordoning off the exterior of the red brick split-level house. He nodded, telling them, "Officer Davis and a couple of the homicide detectives are already here. The victim's body is on the third floor inside the primary bedroom."

Drew gave him a thumbs-up and approached the entrance. He paused, checking for signs of forced entry. Both the door and frame appeared to be completely intact as there were no dents or scrapes. The doorknob and locks looked to be untouched.

Upon entering the living room, Drew noticed that nothing appeared out of place. The eighty-inch television was still mounted on the wall. The pristine pale blue sofa and loveseat hadn't been damaged. All of the crystal vases and copper statues were still standing.

The scent of fresh paint mixed with wood and adhesives filled the air. That new construction smell alerted him that the house may have recently been renovated.

To the right of the living room was the kitchen. The home's open floor plan allowed Drew and Nia to see straight into it. Neither of them could make out a speck of dirt on the white marble countertops, and the stainless steel appliances shone from a distance.

"Why don't we head upstairs and—"

Drew stopped when a man came charging through the front door.

"Where's my wife?" he yelled. "Where is my *wife*?"

Officer Adams grabbed him before he made it to the staircase.

"Sir, I'm gonna need for you to step back outside with me. We'll talk on the front lawn."

The man pushed the officer away, insisting, "Get the hell off of me! I want to see my wife."

Drew and Nia waited until Officer Adams convinced him to leave the house before proceeding up the stairs.

"Poor guy," Nia said. "I wish we could've stopped and talked to him."

"I know. But Adams will handle it. We need to get to the crime scene and find out what we're dealing with here."

Drew's breathing quickened as he heard voices coming

from inside the bedroom at the end of the hallway. He ran his hand along the back of his neck, a stinging heat kindling around his collar.

They approached the doorway. Sunlight streamed through the half-open venetian blinds, brightening the large, airy space. The coppery scent of blood drifted through the air. As officers milled about, Drew noticed that this room, like the others, appeared to be in perfect condition. The grey velvet king-size bed had already been made, with its silver duvet pulled tightly into each corner and the decorative pillows in a precise line along the crystal-tufted headboard.

Not a piece of clothing or pair of shoes was strewn about the floor. A designer handbag was propped along the edge of a mirrored vanity. It looked to be full and the zipper was securely fastened. Next to it was a porcelain Tiffany jewelry tray, which held a pair of diamond earrings, a platinum wedding ring set, a gold Omega watch and a framed photograph.

Drew bent down, staring at the couple in the picture. They were lying on colorful towels at what looked to be a beach resort. The woman's long, curly hair draped down her back. Her head was nestled against the man's chest—the same man who'd just burst through the front door. At the bottom of the photograph was the caption "Living, laughing and loving on our Bahamian honeymoon…"

"Here's a photo of our victim and her husband," Drew said to Nia.

"Sad. Look at them. They appear to be so in love."

"Yes, they do."

He gave the room another once-over. "One thing's for sure. This doesn't look to be a robbery."

"I agree. Nothing looks to be out of place."

Several officers were gathered in the far right corner. "Let's go take a look at the victim," Drew said.

"Right behind you."

As he walked past the bathroom, Drew noticed that the toilet seat was up. He found that odd considering the victim's husband was allegedly away from the home at the time of her murder. In that case, the seat should have been down. He made a mental note to dust it for prints, then approached the crime scene area.

Blood spatter covered the pale gray nightstand and eggshell-colored walls behind the victim. Her hands and feet were bound with duct tape. A deep, jagged gash had been slashed across her throat. An enormous amount of blood had poured from the wound, seeping into the cream Berber carpeting and turning her satin lavender nightgown a deep shade of brown.

"This feels like déjà vu all over again," Nia said. "Our victim looks to have been killed the exact same way as Katie and Violet. She's also petite with dark hair. But again, the big difference is this crime was committed inside her home."

Leaning forward, Drew studied the victim's head. "Hey, take a look at her hair. Notice how long it was in that photo we just saw? According to the date on the picture, it was taken recently. And look at it now. It appears to have been chopped off. Literally."

Nia moved in closer. "Oh my God. It does. You can tell by how uneven the ends are. It doesn't even look to have been cut with scissors. If the assailant did this, he must've used a knife."

"Yeah, the same knife he used to slit her throat, because I can see clumps of dried blood in her hair from here. And look. There are long strands of hair scattered across her body."

"This is so…so *sick*. Is he killing, then collecting souvenirs now, too?"

"Could be. If that's the case, the crimes are escalating. I think our suspect is getting a thrill out of committing these murders—taunting us by leaving clues at the crime scenes and now taking it up a notch. It's like he's daring us to apprehend him before he kills again."

Noticing Officer Davis hovering near the detectives, Drew called out, "Hey, Davis, were you the first one on the scene?"

"I was."

"Who called this in?"

"The neighbor who lives right here on the corner." He motioned to the white-framed casement window, pointing at the house on the left. "The guy told the 9-1-1 operator that he was afraid the victim may be in distress after hearing screams coming through his bathroom window. He let us inside the house, too."

"How'd he let you in?"

"He used a spare key the husband gave him in case of an emergency."

"Did he say why the husband felt it was necessary to give him that key?" Nia asked.

"Yeah, the husband travels a lot for work and his wife is a type 1 diabetic. Since the neighbor is a retired physician, the husband thought it would be a good idea for him to have access to the house in case his wife experienced some sort of health crisis."

"Did you get the impression he had anything to do with this?"

"No, not at all. He appears to be at least seventy-five to

eighty years old. The man was dressed in plaid pajamas, a terry-cloth bathrobe and house slippers when he walked over. It looked as if he'd just rolled out of bed."

"All right," Drew sighed, running his hands along his goatee. "Has anyone called the medical examiner's office yet or do I need to take care of that now?"

"I put in a call as soon as I established that the victim was deceased. She'll be here shortly."

Drew gave him a nod of appreciation. It was the first decent exchange the men had shared since the Katie debacle. "Were you able to walk through the house and see if you could figure out the suspect's point of entry?"

"Not yet. I've been up here helping these guys process the scene."

"Officer Brooks and I will take a look around downstairs, then come back up and see what evidence we can collect."

Giving him a slight nod, Officer Davis inhaled sharply, as if he had something to add. Drew waited for him to continue. But he just stood there awkwardly, his mouth opening and closing several times before he backed away and rejoined the detective.

Drew sensed that he wanted to discuss the Katie situation. Now, however, wasn't the time. He had a case to solve.

"You ready?" he asked Nia before leading her out of the bedroom.

On the way downstairs, the victim's husband could be heard wailing out on the front lawn.

"We need to talk to him before we leave," Drew said. "I wonder how he found out about his wife."

"My guess is that the neighbor called and told him. I've been debating whether he may have had something to do with this. But the way he came tearing through the door with that look of fright on his face? I don't know. Plus he and his wife appeared so happy in that honeymoon photo."

"Not to mention he gave the neighbor a spare key in case his wife experiences a diabetic episode. My gut is telling me that he's not involved."

"Yeah, same."

The pair walked through the living room and back to the family room.

"Another area that appears to be untouched," Drew said, eyeing the row of neatly placed navy pillows lining a tan suede sectional and flat-screen television hanging from the wall.

A wedding photo sat prominently on top of the fireplace mantel. He walked over and stared at the black-and-white picture. The couple was holding hands while running through a grassy meadow. Their smiles radiated through the glass casing. Drew could feel their joy, which vibrated throughout the entire house. Yet today, because of some sick bastard, the lives of the groom, their families and friends would be forever shattered.

"Drew!" Nia called out. "Come and take a look at this."

He approached the sliding glass doors that led out onto the backyard deck.

"This door was unlocked and slightly open. I wonder if the victim forgot to secure it, because nothing appears to have been tampered with or broken. The lock is still intact. This may be how our suspect made his way inside the house."

"Or how he exited. Since there were no signs of forced entry at the front door, there's a possibility that our victim knew the suspect and willingly let him in." Drew knelt down and studied the doorframe. "I wish we could figure out the motive behind these attacks. Why these women? I know they've each got their similarities. Katie and Violet were both single, outgoing and pretty heavy fixtures on the Juniper social scene. But this victim is different. She was married. The murder took place inside her home. What's the connection there?"

"Good question, assuming it's the same killer."

"Exactly. We need to know more about this victim. Starting with her identity. Did you happen to get her name while you were talking with the detectives?"

Nia flipped through the pages in her notebook. "You know, I didn't. We'll find out as soon as we head back up—"

"Hold on," Drew interjected, pointing to the doorframe. "Check this out."

Nia moved in closer as he shone his flashlight toward a partial bloody fingerprint. "Hmm, good catch. I'll see if I can lift an impression of it."

Both officers snapped photos before Nia pulled a bottle from her evidence collection kit.

"What is that you're using?" Drew asked.

"Amido black reagent."

"Nice. That's my preferred chemical of choice for developing blood evidence. I once had a partner who'd use luminol solution, which usually ended up ruining the proteins and genetic markers needed to detect DNA."

"And since luminol is water-based, I bet it diluted the blood impressions, too."

"That's exactly what would happen."

Drew looked on as Nia began applying the reagent to the print. "Where did you learn how to do all this?"

"I minored in forensic science in college and periodically take classes to keep my skills sharp."

"So you always knew you wanted to do this kind of

work, even though you started off in the emergency services department?"

"I did. And working as a 9-1-1 operator gave me a nice head start. Before becoming a police officer, I already had a good understanding of how the radio works, proper protocols, the computer system. Plus I went in knowing how to handle victims and what's expected of law enforcement. Being at that call center really did help prepare me for the streets."

"That's awesome, Brooks. I love hearing about your journey to joining the force." Just as Drew pulled a roll of fingerprint tape from his bag, his cell phone pinged. "Chief Mitchell got held up at the station but he'll be here shortly."

"Good. I'm glad we can report that we've found some evidence. I have never seen him as shaken up as he was today."

"Yeah, neither have I."

Drew looked on as the amido black reagent slowly turned the proteins in the blood a shade of dark blue. Once it had dried, he carefully applied the tape, lifted the print, covered the tape with plastic and placed it inside a brown paper bag.

"That should do it," he told Nia. "Let's head back up and check in with the detectives."

As they walked through the living room, Drew glanced out the window. Officer Adams was still standing on the lawn talking to the victim's husband when the medical examiner's van pulled up. The sight sent the man to his knees. Officer Adams quickly helped him up and sat him inside the squad car.

Drew wished he could do more to ease the husband's sorrow. But there was nothing more important than the task at hand—processing the scene so they could hunt down the killer.

"Hey, Officer Taylor!" Officer Davis called out from the landing. "Can you and Officer Brooks come up here? I need to show you something."

Charging up the stairs, Nia stopped Davis on the way inside the bedroom. "Hey, have you identified the victim yet?"

"I have. Her name is Porter. Ingrid Porter."

"Got it. Thanks."

As Nia began writing the victim's name down in her notepad, Drew noticed her hand freeze on the page.

"What's wrong?" he asked her.

"That name. Ingrid Porter. It sounds so familiar."

"According to one of the detectives," Officer Davis said, "she was born and raised here in Juniper. Maybe you went to school with her or something?"

"That could be it. But I'm not sure…"

"Well, while you try and figure that out, this is what I wanted to show you two."

Officer Davis held up a glossy trifold brochure. Before Drew could make out the wording, his eyes drifted toward the top right side. A single bloody fingerprint was smeared along the edge.

"Hey," he said, pointing toward it. "Did you see that—"

"Wait!" Nia exclaimed, pulling out her cell phone and scrolling through the camera roll. "I remember where I heard that name, Ingrid Porter."

"Where?" Drew and Officer Davis asked in unison.

"She's the woman who got married at the Charlie Sifford Country Club. Look, there's her name on the wedding invitation the killer left at Latimer Park."

Drew stared at the phone screen, tension swirling inside his head. It was all coming together. The invite. The garter. Those clues leading up to Ingrid's murder had nothing to do with the country club itself. They were about the woman getting married there.

"*Damn*," Officer Davis muttered. "Well, now we need to use the clue that was left at this crime scene to figure out the killer's next move."

"Wait, what are you talking about?" Nia asked. "What clue?"

The officer held the brochure in the air again.

"This menu to the Bullseye Bar and Grill."

Chapter Fifteen

Nia awakened to the sound of her pinging cell phone. After yesterday, she had turned the volume all the way up while awaiting Ivy's call. So far, she'd heard nothing and had barely slept.

Opening one eye, Nia grabbed the phone from the nightstand and swiped it open. A text notification appeared on the screen. Finally, a message from her sister.

Hey, sis! Sorry I didn't reach out sooner. The girls and I heard about the latest murder. So tragic! Sounds like she was targeted. No one at Bullseye thinks we're in danger though. STOP worrying about me. I'm good!

Nia sat straight up in bed and replied in all caps.

IVY, THIS IS NOT A JOKE! THE KILLER HAS ALREADY TARGETED ME AND CLEARLY HE KNOWS YOU'RE MY SISTER. SO WHY WOULDN'T HE TARGET YOU?? YOU ARE IN FACT IN DANGER! CALL ME ASAP!!

Nia tossed the phone back onto the nightstand and rolled over. Once her eyes adjusted to the dark room, she gasped, throwing off the comforter. Faint shadows of chairs and floor lamps loomed around her. Nothing looked familiar.

She sucked in a panicked breath, confused by the faint smell of coffee.

A knock at the door sent her shuddering against the headboard. And then, it all came rushing back. Yesterday, after finding out Ingrid Porter was their latest victim, then discovering the Bullseye menu at the crime scene, Nia told Drew she couldn't bear going home alone.

"And you don't have to," he'd told her before gently taking her hand in his. "Not tonight or any other night for that matter. You can stay with me for as long as you want."

Nia remembered the plethora of emotions coursing through her mind. Gratitude spun the fiercest. At this point, the feelings she'd been harboring for Drew had blossomed into something more than just a crush. The sentiments ran deep, fusing a mix of admiration, appreciation and deep attraction.

After processing the crime scene, he'd driven her home and waited patiently while she packed a bag.

"This goes without saying," he had told her while setting up the guest bedroom, "but please, let me reiterate that there is no end date to how long you can stay here. You have an open-ended invitation."

A knock at the door pulled Nia from her thoughts.

"Good morning," Drew called out. "Are you up yet?"

"I am!" she lied. "Just one second…"

Hopping out of bed, Nia slipped on her satin lilac robe, ran her fingers through her tousled curls, then threw open the door.

"Sorry about that. Good morning."

"Hey, I hope you're hungry." He glanced down at the cup of coffee and platter filled with fruit and breakfast breads in his hands. "I didn't know what you'd want to eat, so I went to Cooper's and picked up a little bit of everything."

"I see. That was so thoughtful of you. Thanks."

She took the mug and stepped to the side as he entered the room, placing the platter on the desk. Glancing in the mirror, Nia cringed at her disheveled appearance. The plan was to wake up early, shower and pull herself together before Drew laid eyes on her. Yet here she was, fresh out of bed and looking a rumpled mess. It didn't help that he was fully dressed and perfectly groomed.

"Hey," she began, "do you mind if I freshen up a bit, then we can enjoy breakfast together in the kitchen?"

"Of course!" He grabbed the platter and hurried toward the door. "I'm sorry. I didn't mean to bombard you. I, uh—I guess I got a little overzealous now that you're back in the house. Plus we had such a rough day yesterday, so I figured an early breakfast would be nice. And…well, now I'm just rambling. But you get the gist of what I'm trying to say."

"I do. I appreciate it. *And* you."

As Drew hovered in the doorway, Nia couldn't help but smile. His thoughtfulness, albeit a bit awkward, was quite endearing. "I won't be long getting ready."

"That's fine," he said, glancing down at his watch. "We've got plenty of time before we're due at the station." He turned to walk out, then took a step back. "Hey, were you ever able to get ahold of Ivy?"

Rolling her eyes, Nia went over to the nightstand and grabbed her phone. "Yes, *finally*. But not until a few minutes ago. She and her coworkers are safe. Of course she blew off my warning. Ivy still isn't taking any of this seriously. I'm telling you, the girl thinks she's invincible, just like she always has. She's the type who believes the universe will keep her covered."

"Yeah, well, this time she really needs to take heed. I hope you can get through to her."

The pair fell silent, Drew's gaze remaining on Nia as he stepped into the hallway.

"I'll leave you to it."

The moment he closed the door, Nia hurried to the bathroom and put a rush on her morning routine. While she made it into the kitchen in less than forty-five minutes, it looked as though she'd taken much longer to pull herself together after putting a little extra care into applying her makeup and flat-ironing soft waves into her hair.

"I just received an email from the crime lab," Drew said once she took a seat at the table. "There was no DNA evidence found on those wind chimes in your backyard or the garter. I'm guessing the suspect must've worn gloves."

"That makes sense. But if he wore gloves then, why wouldn't he have used them while committing the murders?"

"Maybe he did. Think about the method he used to murder the victims. This guy is extremely violent. So violent that he could've worn gloves and torn them while performing the acts."

Nia nodded, spreading her plain bagel with strawberry cream cheese. "You make a good point."

"We'll see what comes of the fingerprint evidence taken from this latest crime scene. Until then, let's keep working with what we've got. Violet Shields's phone records should be coming in any minute now that Officer Mills has submitted the warrant to the carrier. As for Ingrid's cell phone, we got lucky after finding it inside her purse. Mills is going to start downloading the data today."

"You know, I had a theory that all these murders were linked to the Someone for Everyone app. But Ingrid was married. So I doubt she's connected to the killer in that way."

"Yeah, well, you never know…"

Flipping her notepad open to the most recent bulleted list, Nia asked, "What do you mean?"

"I mean, stranger things have happened. People do have affairs, flings, no-strings-attached types of situationships. Hell, a lot of people use those dating apps for quickie one-night stands."

"Something's telling me that's not the case here. But like you said, you never know. I can't help but think about Ingrid's husband though. He was so distraught over her murder. News that she was being unfaithful would tear him apart."

Nia lurched in her chair when Drew jumped up and began pacing the floor.

"What's going on?" she asked. "What are you doing?"

"I just thought of something." He picked up his cell phone and began typing away.

"Um, are you gonna tell me what you thought of?"

"I will," he said, placing the cell back down, then refilling their coffee mugs. "Just let me see what comes of this first."

Within seconds, his phone buzzed. Drew almost knocked it off the table trying to grab it.

"I'm dying to know what you're up to," Nia said, craning her neck to get a look at the cell.

As his eyes darted across the screen, he yelled, "Bingo! See, that's exactly what I thought."

"*What's* exactly what you thought?"

"I just sent a message to Ingrid's husband asking how he and his wife met. I'll give you one guess as to what he responded."

Pressing her palm against her forehead, she rasped, "If I were to say through the Someone for Everyone app…"

"Then you would be absolutely right."

"*Drew*," Nia shrieked, hopping up and throwing her arms around him. "You are a genius! So Ingrid was on the app, too. See, now we *really* need for Someone for Everyone to turn over the victims' membership information."

"Agreed. It's just a matter of time now that Officer Ryan has filed a motion to compel their objection to the court. At this point, I'm almost certain the administrators have something to hide."

"Not only that, but I'm sure they don't wanna deal with the controversy of having a member who's a serial killer. Whatever the case may be, this is good. We've now got a common thread linking two of our three victims. We'll see what comes of Violet's cell phone data once it comes in."

Drew quickly sobered up as he slumped back down in his chair. "You mean three out of four. Because unfortunately, you're now included on that list."

IT WAS A little after 1:00 p.m. when Nia and Drew settled in at a table in the back of the Bullseye Bar and Grill. The place was packed with lunchtime patrons as almost every rustic table and booth was filled. Industrial fans whirled from the high exposed ceiling. Jumbo flat-screen televisions hung from each wall, showing practically every sporting event from basketball to soccer to tennis. Nooks hidden within the wood-paneled walls housed dartboards, pinball machines, foosball tables and cornhole boards.

Nia wished she were there for the honey-glazed wings, frothy mugs of beer and a round of pool. But she and Drew were on a stakeout of sorts, looking to see who'd drift in and out during Ivy's shift.

While she tried not to appear as worried as she felt, Nia was actually terrified for her sister. She hoped that by showing up to the bar in person, Ivy would take heed of the danger she was in—especially after refusing to call Nia back that morning.

Sis, you're really killing my vibe, Ivy had texted shortly before Nia arrived at the station. *If I wanted to live my life in fear while constantly looking over my shoulder, I would've just stayed in LA!*

Nia asked what in the world that last statement meant as Ivy never told her she was fearful of anything back in LA. Of course the question went unanswered. Typical Ivy—full of secrets and short on admissions.

"Will you look at this girl?" Nia said to Drew while pointing toward the bar. "Ivy is back there just laughing and joking as if she doesn't have a care in the world."

"Well, in Ivy's mind, she doesn't. But that's part of the reason why we're here. Hopefully our presence will prove to her that this is a serious matter, and she needs to move with caution."

"I highly doubt that's gonna happen. She seems to think we're here on a social call. The way she was introducing us to everybody when we walked in, as if we're her guests of honor as opposed to two police officers investigating a serial killer…" Nia paused, grazing her nails against her palms while watching Ivy wiggle her hips as she shook a Boston Shaker high in the air. "She needs to grow up and understand that it's gonna take more than just good vibes and a positive aura to help keep her safe."

"Hey, you never know. Maybe that'll work for her."

"Please tell me you don't believe in all those woo-woo theories, too."

Drew reached inside his beige utility jacket, playfully digging around. "I might. Let me grab my tarot deck and pull a few cards. See what they have to say about all this."

When Nia's expression twisted in frustration, he said, "Look, I get it. You're worried about your sister. But I'm just trying to lighten the mood because there isn't much you can do about her behavior. Just as you've stated time and time again, you cannot control Ivy. All you can do is advise her, which is exactly what you're doing."

"I know, I know." She picked up her fork and stabbed at her Caesar salad, no longer in the mood to eat. Thoughts of her sister becoming the next victim had ruined her appetite.

Glancing around the restaurant, Drew said, "Have you noticed anybody looking suspicious?"

"Yeah, how about everybody in here!" Nia quipped, only half joking.

Her gaze fell on a young man sitting at the bar who was there when she and Drew arrived. He was tall and lean, appearing well-groomed with his freshly trimmed Caesar haircut and goatee. When Nia walked past him, she'd noticed his half-eaten bowl of pasta, indicating he had been there for a while.

"What about that guy?" she asked Drew, pointing at the man as he stood on his stool's footrest and leaned over the bar.

"Which guy?"

"The one in the navy blazer and khaki chinos. He's giving me narcissistic, former frat boy vibes with the constant high-fiving and shoulder bouncing whenever a new song comes on."

"Oh, yeah. I noticed him when we first walked in. He definitely likes attention. I picked up more of a former collegiate athlete, still-living-in-his-glory-days type of vibe off him."

"Either way, something seems off. He's doing entirely too much. And of course my sister, who is a douchebag magnet, has been entertaining him the whole time we've been here."

Nia watched as Ivy rocked her hips back and forth, then poured the shaker's contents into a martini glass. When she slid it toward the man, he blew her a kiss, causing Nia to almost choke on a slice of grilled chicken.

"You know," she said, "when Ivy first got back to town, I told her to be careful and watch who she buddies up with. And look at her. Entertaining every man sitting at the bar. Especially the one who looks like the Preppy Killer."

Tapping his finger against Ingrid's police report, Drew replied, "Well, on a positive note, maybe she can give us some much needed intel since we're not getting anywhere with the evidence that's been left at these crime scenes."

"That would be nice. Notice I didn't even get my hopes up when it came to that bloody fingerprint on the Bullseye menu recovered from Ingrid's crime scene. And just as we'd suspected, it belonged to Ingrid."

"Yep. Another taunt aimed at us. As for Ingrid's husband, Terrance, Officer Adams's notes confirmed that he has a solid alibi. He was at work at the time of her murder."

"And I know the neighbor's officially been ruled out, too. What about the Ring camera footage? I noticed the cameras over the front and back doors. Any word from Terrance on that?"

"Another dead end," Drew grumbled. "Terrance told Officer Adams that the Wi-Fi got really spotty around the time of their home renovation. Plus he and Ingrid were in the process of upgrading the security system. So for the time being, the service was down."

"We need to talk to the neighbors then. See if their cameras captured any footage."

"Officer Adams was on top of that. While we were processing the scene, he interviewed the neighbors to find out if they saw or heard anything. We'll follow up with him once we get back to the station—"

Drew was interrupted when Ivy came strolling over to the table. She plopped down in the seat next to Nia's and planted a kiss on her cheek.

"Hey, big sis!" she squealed, her words a bit slurred. "Hey, big sis's partner."

Nia held her hand to her nose. "*Ivy.* I know that isn't alcohol I smell on your breath. It's barely lunchtime!"

Ivy giggled, tilting her head to one side. "Oopsies… You've got Gene to blame for that. He and I have been taking shots of whiskey ever since he got here. You know how it is. Hashtag that bartender life!"

"Yeah, how about hashtag you need to slow down," Nia rebutted. "I'm guessing Gene is the guy sitting at the bar who's been vying for your attention ever since we got here?"

"Yep, that's him. Isn't he cute?" She turned and wiggled her fingers at him. He immediately hopped up and began making his way toward them. "No!" Ivy called out, gesturing for him to sit back down. "I'm taking care of some business here. I'll be back soon. Just give me a few minutes!"

He tossed her an exaggerated scowl before returning to his stool.

"Ivy," Nia began, "listen to me. This serial killer investigation is not a joke. Things are really heating up and I'm gonna need for you to start taking your safety more seriously. Now, I'm glad you're staying away from my house. But as for all these wild late nights, the drinking, the taking up with strangers—it's got to stop."

"I agree," Drew chimed in, his eyes softening with concern as he stared across the table at Ivy. "I don't know if your sister has shared this with you, but if not, I trust that you'll keep it to yourself as we can't risk compromising the investigation. But at this latest crime scene, the killer left a Bullseye menu near the victim's body."

"What?" Ivy shrieked so loudly that several patrons turned and stared. "Nia, why didn't you tell me that?"

"When did I have a chance to? I've been trying to reach you since last night, but you refused to call me back!"

Nia looked to Drew, silently urging him to interject before her exchange with Ivy turned into a full-blown argument. He gave her a discreet wink before jumping in.

"Ivy, Nia and I aren't trying to scare you. We just wanna warn you that the streets aren't safe. Your sister is one of the lead investigators on this case, and thanks to all the news media coverage, I'm sure everyone in the community knows that. She's become a target. That Bullseye menu left at the crime scene indicates you may be one as well."

"Oh my God," Ivy moaned, her head falling onto Nia's shoulder.

"Remember when you first got back to town?" Nia asked. "And I told you that Juniper is a different place than it was when you left? Well, this is why. So just watch yourself. Cut out the late nights. Don't go out alone. Be more private on social media. And if you're doing any online dating, cancel your memberships. At least until we get this maniac locked up."

"Yeah!" someone yelled loudly.

Nia watched as the guy at the bar Ivy had been talking to jumped up from his stool and pumped his fist in the air. "Let's go, Buffaloes!"

"What is his deal?" Drew asked.

"He played college football and he's a huge sports fan."

"So he's a friend of yours?"

"We're getting to know one another. He's actually a talent scout in the music industry, and he promised to help me book a few gigs around town. Maybe even something big at one of the venues in Denver. Starting with, drumroll please, the Rose Theater."

"The Rose Theater?" Nia echoed skeptically.

"Yes. The famed Rose Theater, better known as the venue that can make or break a performer's career."

"Um, Ivy?" Drew chimed in. "You do know that place has been under renovation for months, and it may not re-open for another year or so."

"Oh, really?"

"Yes, really," Nia replied, tossing her sister a tight side-eye. "I can't believe you actually fell for the game this man is running on you."

"I didn't fall for anything, little Miss Paranoia. What, you think I just took him at his word? I did do some re-search. And after looking Gene up, I saw that he has some pretty notable credits to his name. But anyway," Ivy con-tinued quickly before Nia could inquire about said credits, "I'd better get back to work. Oh! And before I forget, Gene is trying to get me on the schedule to perform at Army and Lou's new artists' night next weekend. If he does, you two have to promise me that you'll come."

Drew looked toward Nia, who was slow to respond.

"Pleeease?" Ivy begged, pressing her hands together. "It would mean the world to me. If I get this, it'll be the first real singing gig I've booked in…in *months*. I could really use the support."

"Well, after all that," Nia told her, "how can I say no? Now I can't speak for Drew, but of course I'll be there."

"Nope," he said. "You can speak for me on this one. Because I'll be there, too. As a matter of fact, I wouldn't miss it."

Despite talking directly to Ivy, Drew's eyes were on Nia. She could tell by the glint in his gaze that he knew this was important to her. She mouthed the words *thank you* before turning back to her sister.

"So then it's settled. We'll see you next weekend at Army and Lou's."

"*If* I book the gig."

"*When* you book the gig," Nia assured her before glancing at the time. "Listen, it was good seeing you, and I'm really glad we had a chance to talk. But Drew and I should probably get back to the station. We've got a lot of work to do."

"So soon?" Ivy whined.

"Yes, ma'am. As much as we'd love to spend the day here watching sports and playing foosball, we've got a number of murders to solve."

"Ivy," Drew said, handing her his credit card, "it was nice to finally meet you, and thank you for everything."

"It was nice meeting you, too, you're welcome, and please, put that credit card away. Your money is no good here."

"No, Ivy," Nia said. "You don't have to do that."

"Nope. Everything is on the house. Family eats and drinks for free. Now get out of here and go solve your case."

After saying their goodbyes, Nia noticed Drew slip a fifty-dollar bill inside Ivy's hand. She tossed him a wink of thanks, then headed toward the door.

On the way out she gave Ivy's friend Gene one last glance, searching his eyes for that cold, blank look she'd seen in so many killers' mug shots. He didn't have it. When Ivy walked back behind the bar and leaned toward him, he gently covered her hands with his, giving her a bright smile that appeared sweet and genuine.

"So what are you thinking about your sister's acquaintance?" Drew asked.

"I don't think he's our guy."

"Neither do I."

As the pair climbed inside the car, their phones pinged simultaneously.

"Uh-oh," Drew uttered. "Can you check your cell and see what's happening?"

"Yep. It's an email from Officer Mills." Nia swiped open the message. "Oh, *wooow...*"

"What's going on?"

"Violet Shields's cell phone data just came in."

"And?"

"She was an active member on the Someone for Everyone app."

Chapter Sixteen

"Drew!" Nia called out from the guest room.

"What's up?"

"Did I tell you that Ivy texted me about ten times today, reminding me about her show tonight?"

"You did. And you know what I say? Let the woman have her moment. This evening means a lot to her."

Drew fastened his slim-cut gray slacks, leaving unsaid that he was just as excited for the night as Ivy, if not more so.

Toward the end of the week, Ivy had shared the news that she'd booked the gig at Army and Lou's. Tonight would mark the first occasion that he and Nia were getting dressed up and enjoying some time together away from the station in an official social capacity.

The past several days had been nothing short of chaotic. After Ingrid Porter's murder hit the news, Chief Mitchell was forced into defense mode, appearing on every local news channel to discuss the case. The department had been accused of being inadequate and inefficient. The towns-people were insisting they bring in the FBI. A couple of outlets and podcasters even portrayed Drew and Nia as being a pair of bumbling idiots who were being outwitted by their suspect.

The pressure to solve the case was getting to everyone.

But no two officers were more affected by the insults and scrutiny than Drew and Nia. At first, she'd told Ivy that they couldn't make it to her show, feeling as though the evening would be better spent working the case. But Drew quickly reminded her that she was still a human being. Focusing on the investigation 24/7 wasn't healthy. Together, he and Nia had put in enough hours that week alone to fill up a month's worth of work for some officers. So when Ivy messaged Nia asking if she'd changed her mind, Drew insisted that Nia RSVP for them both.

After throwing on his blazer, Drew spritzed a few pumps of cologne on his neck, then headed to the living room. Of course he'd beaten Nia there. She had been groaning for the past hour and a half about how she couldn't figure out what to wear and that it was a bad hair day.

Drew blew her off, knowing she was exaggerating. Since Nia had been staying at his place, he'd seen firsthand just how many items of clothing she owned. And when it came to her hair, it didn't matter whether she had it wrapped in a bun or flowing freely over her shoulders. Either way she always managed to look beautiful.

"Nia!" he called out, glancing at his watch. "We're gonna be late. It's already past seven o'clock. Isn't your sister going on at eight?"

"Yes, she is!"

"Well, we'd better get a move on. I'd like to get a good table and order a bottle of champagne before the show starts."

"Ivy already reserved a table for us up front. We'll be sitting in the VIP section, where there's bottle service."

"Ooh," Drew uttered, strolling over to the gold-framed mirror in the hallway and giving himself another once-over. "All right then. Fancy…"

The moment he heard high heels clicking across the floor, Drew spun around, stretching his neck as Nia rushed into the living room. When she came into view, he almost fell against the wall.

While he'd expected her to look nice, he had *not* expected all of this. She was wearing a black strapless leather dress that stopped somewhere in the middle of her thighs. The outfit showcased every ample curve on her slender body. Her hair had been pulled back into a sleek ponytail, and sparkly dangling earrings shimmered along her delicate neck. Her matte red lipstick set the look off, as did the silver stilettos with straps that snaked around her ankles.

"You… I—I think you look…" Drew stammered, completely lost for words.

"I know, I know," Nia said, hurrying over to the coatrack and pulling down a sheer floor-length duster. "I'm late. But I ended up having to throw my hair into this ponytail because it kept frizzing. And the dress I'd originally wanted to wear is at my house, so I had to settle on this one. I hope it doesn't look too snug. And these *shoes*… This is the first time I've ever worn them, so I'm gonna try my best not to waddle around like a walrus when I walk—"

"Nia," he interrupted, taking the duster out of her hands and helping her into it. "You look stunning. Absolutely stunning."

She turned to him, her frazzled look spreading into a slight grin. "I do?"

"Yes. You do. Trust me, you're going to be the most beautiful woman there."

Drew stopped himself. Had he gone too far? Said too much?

Just as he thought to apologize, Nia kissed him softly

on the cheek and whispered, "Thank you," confirming that the last thing he needed to be was sorry.

"Just stating the facts," he mumbled, relishing the scent of rose perfume radiating from her neck.

On the way to the car, he couldn't control his ogling as his eyes traveled every inch of her body. His teeth clenched when the stir in his groin responded to the sight. While her hips swayed to the rhythm of her sexy walk, he wondered how much longer he could suppress his growing desire for her.

DREW PULLED OPEN Army and Lou's frosted glass door and followed Nia inside. The moment she gave the hostess her name, they were led down the long wood-paneled hallway lined with black-and-white photos of all the jazz greats who'd performed there over the years.

They stepped down into the dimly lit, intimate main room of the club where the featured performers appeared. The place was already packed as every table and seat at the bar was occupied.

"Follow me to the stage!" the hostess shouted over the house band that was playing a rendition of John Coltrane's "Naima." "Ivy made sure we got you all set up in the VIP area. Once you're seated, the server will be over to take your food and drink orders."

Drew's breath caught in his throat when Nia reached back and grabbed his hand. Practically every man's head turned in her direction as they made their way through the crowded club. Admittedly, it felt good being by her side. And just as he'd told her, Nia was by far the most beautiful woman in the club.

A server approached the table the moment they were seated. Drew ordered champagne and a couple of appetizers to start. If she was up for it, he planned on taking Nia somewhere else for a nice, quiet dinner afterwards.

"I am so excited!" she said, pressing her hands against her voluptuous chest. "I haven't seen Ivy perform in years. Whenever she'd land a gig here or in LA, I was always too busy with work to attend. So tonight is really special." She slid her arm across the black bistro table and clasped Drew's hand. "Especially with you being here. Thanks again for coming with me. It means a lot. I wouldn't have wanted to be here alone because…you know."

"I do know. You don't have to thank me. Being here with you is my pleasure. And I'm happy to support your sister's dream. Plus, like I said before, we both needed a night out. This case is getting to us both, and—"

Nia held her finger to his lips. "*Shh.* You can't do that. You're going against the rules. We're not supposed to discuss the investigation tonight. Remember?"

As her skin pressed against his mouth, Drew resisted the urge to grab her hand and kiss it. "You're right. I'll drop it."

The moment was interrupted when Cynthia and a couple of other 9-1-1 operators approached the table. After chatting for several minutes, Drew tapped open his phone's home screen. It was six minutes to eight o'clock.

He tapped Nia's thigh, then pointed toward the stage. "It's almost showtime…"

"I know!" she gushed, bursting into rapid applause.

When the server came over with their champagne and appetizers, Cynthia and the others said their goodbyes, then hurried back to their table. Nia picked up a glass and held it in the air.

"To Ivy's performance tonight. May it be amazing and lead to all her dreams coming true. And…to us. May we continue to fight the good fight until we catch the killer."

Drew smirked, clinking his glass against Nia's. "I would do to you what you did to me and press my finger against your lips considering you just brought up the investigation. But I won't. I don't wanna ruin your lipstick."

"How thoughtful of you," she teased, blowing a kiss in his direction before taking a sip of her drink.

You'd better cut it out, he almost warned, realizing the evening was bringing out another side of Nia. Thoughts of how it would end ruminated as he readjusted his pants leg.

When the music slowed, Nia reached underneath the table and gave his thigh a squeeze. "This is it. It's time for Ivy's performance!"

While she peered at the stage his eyes remained on her. Drew waited for Nia's hand to slip from his leg. It didn't.

"Okay," she said. "It's after eight now. Where is Ivy?"

"Maybe she's still getting ready, or—"

He paused when a woman came running out from behind a curtain. He'd expected for it to be Ivy. It wasn't.

The woman rushed to the stage and whispered something in the bandleader's ear. He nodded, then pulled the microphone off the stand.

"Good evening, ladies and gentlemen! Welcome to Army and Lou's sizzling Saturday night showcase!"

The crowd broke into applause. Nia wiggled in her seat, then raised her hands in the air, clapping louder than anyone around them.

"If Ivy is peeking out into the audience from backstage," she said, "I want her to see me cheering. You know, just in case she's got the jitters."

"You're such a good big sister," Drew said with a wink before turning his attention back to the man on the mic.

"Thank you for coming out tonight. We've got a roster full of extremely talented artists ready to perform for you. So prepare for some intoxicating rhythm, boisterous blues, vivacious vocals and hypnotic harmonies. First up on tonight's schedule *was* the lovely, talented Ivy Brooks."

"Was?" Nia uttered. "What does he mean, *was*?"

"But I've just been informed that Ivy has yet to arrive. So we're gonna move on to our next rising star, Mario King, then bring Ivy up later tonight. Mario, come on out here and show the people what you've got, my man!"

"Drew, did I just hear him correctly? Ivy isn't here?"

"That's what he said. Maybe she got caught up at work and is running late."

"Nooo..." Snatching open her clutch, Nia pulled out her cell phone. "Ivy wouldn't have missed this for the world. It's all she's been talking about this week. Plus she took the day off. She wanted to make sure she was at the sound check on time this afternoon. She'd even mentioned staying here until tonight so that she wouldn't be late for the show."

"Has she called or texted you?"

"No, not since early this afternoon." Nia turned in her chair, frantically searching the club. "I wonder if any of her friends from Bullseye are here. And that guy who booked this gig for her. What was his name? Gene? He's supposed to be here, too. Have you seen him?"

Drew peered out at all the unfamiliar faces. "No, I haven't."

When Nia jumped up and rushed through the crowd, Drew tossed some cash onto the table and followed her. She stopped at the hostess stand.

"Excuse me," she said to the woman who'd seated them. "Are you involved in scheduling the artists' performances or arranging the sound checks?"

"I am. I keep track of the calendar for the manager. You two were guests of Ivy Brooks, right?"

"Right. She's my sister. Her sound check was scheduled for this afternoon, and she was supposed to perform at eight o'clock. But the bandleader just said that she's not here."

The hostess opened a brown vinyl planner and flipped through the pages. "Hold on. Let me take a look at today's sign-in sheet."

Sensing that Nia was on the brink of breaking down, Drew wrapped an arm around her. "Try and stay calm. I'm sure Ivy is fine. It's been a long time since she's performed. Maybe her nerves got the best of her and she had a change of heart."

"I doubt that. Ivy doesn't get nervous to the point where she wouldn't show up. My sister is the most confident woman I know. Believe me, she wouldn't have let anything get in the way of being here tonight. Unless…"

As her voice trailed off, dread pounded Drew's frontal lobe. In his ten-plus years of being a police officer, that all-too-familiar sensation meant one thing—something was wrong.

"Here she is," the hostess said, pointing at one of the appointments scribbled inside the calendar. "Ivy Brooks. Her sound check was scheduled for two o'clock. But she didn't show up."

Drew felt Nia lean further into him. He held her tighter before asking the hostess, "Did she call and try to reschedule?"

"No. Which I thought was strange after she'd called several times throughout the week just to confirm she was still on tonight's roster. But no one here at the club has heard from her at all today."

Pulling Drew toward the exit, Nia shouted, "We need to find my sister!"

Chapter Seventeen

It had been nine days since Ivy went missing.

After Nia and Drew left Army and Lou's, they'd rushed to Bullseye, praying that Ivy had had a change of heart and gone to work. But they were told that she never showed up. On the way out the pair ran into Madison. She hadn't seen Ivy since she'd left the apartment earlier that day.

Despite Madison having just left home, Nia begged Madison to take them back to her place. She needed to see for herself that Ivy wasn't there. When they arrived, Nia and Drew spoke to the landlord and learned that the building had no security cameras. None of the buildings in the area looked to have any, either.

Once inside Madison's unit, the officers searched every corner of the cramped one bedroom. There was no sign of Ivy.

Before leaving, Nia went through her sister's things. She'd found a duffel bag filled with what looked to be the things Ivy had planned on taking to the club the day of her performance—a slinky red floor-length gown, makeup bag, curling iron and rollers. Packs of peppermint and chamomile tea to soothe her throat. Her journal.

What was most alarming was the sight of her keys, wallet and cell phone. Ivy never would've left the apartment without those essential items.

That's when Nia and Drew rang the alarm. They issued an alert with Juniper PD as well as the surrounding areas, informing the agencies that it was likely her sister had been kidnapped.

"Hey," Drew said, "how are you holding up?"

Nia jumped at the sound of his voice.

"Sorry," he continued, slowly entering her cubicle and placing a brown paper bag on the desk. "I didn't mean to scare you."

"You're fine. It's me. I've been so jumpy that any little noise sends me leaping ten feet in the air."

"I know. Which is why I've been stuck to your side twenty-four seven ever since Ivy…"

"Went missing," Nia finished for him, struggling to sound stronger than she felt.

He took a seat, propping his chin in his hands while studying her expression. "You're doing it again."

"Doing what?"

"Getting in your feelings. Shuffling through everything you think you've done wrong or could've done differently. Stay out of the weeds, Nia. Fly above it all and keep your head in the now." He pointed toward the bag. "Since you refuse to step away from your desk for food these days, I picked up a turkey club and cup of tomato soup for you from Cooper's. You won't be any good in the search for your sister if you don't start taking better care of yourself."

"I know. But food is the last thing on my mind right now. I'm already sick to my stomach at the thought of what happened to her. Or the idea that she might be—"

"Held captive somewhere," Drew interjected firmly. "And I get that. But still. At least try and take a couple of sips of soup while we go over the recent developments. Chief Mitchell wants an update on the case this afternoon."

Nia reached inside the bag and pulled out the sandwich. The scent of freshly cooked bacon drifted from the foil wrapping. Normally that would've sent hunger pains rumbling through her gut. Today it triggered a bout of nausea.

"So," Drew said, opening his well-worn composition notebook. "Here's what we've got for the chief so far. The rest of the DNA evidence found at Ingrid Porter's house came back from the lab. The fingerprints lifted from the sliding glass door and toilet seat matched that of the suspect's we found at the other victims' crime scenes. After running it through the database once again, we still didn't get a hit."

"Got it," Nia said, typing the notes into her computer as Drew spoke.

"We looked into that guy, Gene, who booked the singing gig for Ivy. His fingerprints didn't match the suspect's, plus he has a solid alibi."

"Right. He'd spent the day with his wife and newborn baby, and wasn't able to leave the house the night of Ivy's performance. Should I add the part where he's a sleazy bastard who was hitting on my sister even though he's married, and—"

"Hold on," Drew cut in. "You're not wrong. But we should probably leave those particulars out of the report."

"If you insist."

Nia continued typing, acting as if she was actually adding the details to the document. When Drew broke into a deep, throaty chuckle, she couldn't help but laugh.

"Wait, is that a smile I see on your face?" he asked. "And did I just hear an actual giggle escape those lips?"

"Yes, you did. You've somehow managed to make even the hardest moments more bearable. That's one of the things I love most about you."

"Ooh, there are things you love about me? Wow, Officer Brooks. You just made my day."

A palpable energy swirled between the pair as they both fell silent. Just when Drew reached for Nia's hand, she cleared her throat and turned back to the computer. "All right, what else have we got?"

Slouching against the back of his chair, he responded, "The court granted our motion to compel Someone for Everyone's objection to the subpoena. So the administrators have no choice but to comply by the deadline."

"Okay, I've got that recorded. Anything else?"

Drew blew a pensive sigh. "Lastly, we need to tell Chief Mitchell everything that you found inside Ivy's journal." He slammed his notebook shut. "But first, you should probably start by telling me."

After saving the document, Nia grabbed the diary and shifted in her seat. She hated having gone through something of her sister's that was so personal. Reading her innermost thoughts and private actions, let alone sharing them with Drew and Chief Mitchell, felt like a betrayal of their sisterhood. But Nia had no choice now that Ivy had gone missing. This was a matter of life and death. And she was willing to do whatever it took to get her sister back.

Nia turned to one of the pages she'd bookmarked with a pink sticky note. "Okay, so, I'll just give you a brief overview of what Ivy had going on back in LA, because I think some of this had a lot to do with why she left the city so abruptly."

"All right," Drew said, cracking open his notebook again and jotting down notes. "I'm listening."

"Earlier this year, Ivy started working for an elite men's social club called Legacy. Have you heard of it?"

"No, I haven't. What's it about?"

"It's basically an underground secret society of sorts. Membership consists of prestigious business owners, judges, attorneys, investment bankers—you get the idea. It's like a brotherhood. These men meet up and unwind over top-shelf spirits, expensive cigars and high stakes poker games while debating politics and brokering business deals."

"Interesting. What type of work was Ivy doing for the club?"

"She was just bartending as far as I know. But the thing is, Ivy was being paid a lot of money. In cash. That part makes sense, because I never could figure out how she'd managed to pay rent on a two-bedroom apartment in a Beverly Hills high-rise. The question is, was she making all that money just serving drinks? Or was there more to it than that?"

"Good question. Because the average bartender definitely isn't making enough money to live in that area."

"Exactly." Nia flipped to a page that had been bookmarked with a yellow sticky note. "I'm thinking that the members were throwing a lot of money at the women who worked for the club as a way of grooming them. Hoping the professional rapport would grow into something more."

"Was there anything in Ivy's journal that gave you that impression?"

"Well, a few months into the job, she'd mentioned that the club's dynamics started to change. Some of the patrons' behavior became dodgy and demanding. Their requests went from business to personal. There was one man in particular whose actions had become downright inappropriate with his aggressive flirting and pleas for a date. I looked through the entire journal for his name, but Ivy never mentioned it. She only referred to him as The Donor."

"The Donor," Drew repeated, rapidly taking notes, then

biting down on the tip of his pen. "I wonder if he was one of her big tippers."

"That's what I'm thinking. One name that Ivy did mention pretty often is Coco. She's someone who also worked for Legacy. I found her contact information in Ivy's cell phone and left her a voicemail message. Hopefully she'll get back to me soon. But in the meantime, that's what I've got."

"That's a good amount of information to work with. At least we have a substantial report to turn in to the chief and some solid leads to look into." Drew tossed his notebook onto the desk and slid closer to Nia. "Listen, I know things are tough right now, but I want you to stay positive. And trust that we're going to find your sister."

She nodded, unable to verbally respond for fear that a fresh batch of tears would start to fall.

"Ready to go meet with Chief Mitchell?" Drew asked.

After taking a couple of swallows of soup, Nia gathered herself, then stood. "Yes. I'm ready."

NIA INCREASED THE volume on her cell phone and set it in the middle of the coffee table. She and Drew were sitting on his couch with the latest episode of "Black Cake" muted and their bowls of shrimp risotto only half-eaten.

Their evening had been interrupted when Ivy's coworker Coco finally returned Nia's call.

"So this men's group, Legacy," Drew said. "It isn't based in just one state?"

"No, it isn't," Coco replied. "The members live in California, Nevada, Arizona and Colorado. And they meet in major cities throughout those states. That's what makes the group so difficult to trace."

"Got it," Nia said. "Now, let's get back to Ivy. If she was

dealing with all this harassment from the members, well, one member in particular, why didn't she just quit the job?"

"Because the money was too good. But then something happened, and the president of the club fired her. Since she and I were so close, I ended up getting fired, too."

Nia threw Drew a look before he asked, "When you say something happened, what exactly do you mean?"

"I, um… What I mean is, she knew too much."

"What exactly did she know?"

The other end of the phone went silent.

"Coco?" Nia said. "Are you still there?"

"Yeah, I'm here. I just… I really don't feel comfortable talking about this over the phone."

"Well, is there any way we could meet up in person?"

Another long pause.

"Did she hang up?" Drew whispered just as Coco's low grunt rumbled through the speaker.

"Look," she said, "that's not possible. I'm leaving for New Mexico tomorrow night. I've gotta get out of here. After what's happened to Ivy, I just don't feel safe anymore."

Clenching her teeth together, Nia willed herself to keep pressing. "Where are you now?"

"At my parents' cabin in Lake Astor."

"What if we meet you there, before you leave town?" Drew suggested. "I promise that we won't take up too much of your time."

Nia slid to the edge of the couch, balling her hands into tight fists while awaiting the response.

After what seemed like forever, Coco finally uttered, "Fine. Be here tomorrow at two o'clock sharp. I won't have much time to spare. I'll give you thirty minutes, tops."

"Thank you, Coco," Nia told her, grabbing the phone and

swiping open the Notes app. "You have no idea how much this means to us. Where is the cabin locate—"

"I'll text you the address."

Before they could say another word, Coco disconnected the call.

"All righty, then," Drew said, staring at the phone screen. "I certainly hope she's more helpful than that tomorrow."

Collapsing against the back of the couch, Nia rubbed her tired eyes. "It's fine. I get it. She's frustrated and obviously scared. I'm just glad that she agreed to meet with us and pray that whatever she knows will lead us to Ivy."

Drew glanced at the clock, then picked up their bowls. "It's getting late. I'm sure you're probably exhausted. Why don't we head to bed? We've got a big day tomorrow."

"I'm right behind you."

Nia turned off the television and grabbed their glasses. On the way to the kitchen, she noticed a slight spring in her step, driven by a boost of optimism. The call with Coco felt like more than just another empty possibility. It seemed like a tangible tip.

After straightening up, she and Drew headed down the hallway, stopping in front of the guest bedroom.

"You were great today," he said. "We're making good progress."

"Thanks. Just ten minutes ago I was feeling so confident. But now all of a sudden I'm starting to worry about tomorrow. What if Coco gets cold feet and decides she doesn't want to tell us anything? Or what if she skips town before we can even get to Lake Astor—"

"Nia," Drew interrupted, taking her hands in his. "None of those things are going to happen. Coco gave us her word and I believe she'll come through. She and Ivy are close friends. She wants her to be found just as badly as we do. So just relax. Don't put all that unnecessary stress on yourself by running a bunch of fake scenarios through your head."

"You know I have a bad habit of doing that. And I know I need to stop."

Drew leaned in and gently kissed her forehead. Closing her eyes, Nia's hands skimmed his broad shoulders, then rested against the back of his neck. The feel of his lips against her skin was comforting, rousing a stir of emotions deep within her.

The moment intensified when Drew slipped his arms around her waist. As his body pressed against hers, she felt a bulge against her thigh.

Abruptly pulling away, he muttered, "We, uh…we'd better get some rest."

Nia didn't respond, while eyeing Drew intently. Nothing in his lingering stare indicated he wanted to leave.

He brushed several strands of hair away from her face. "I hope you sleep well."

"You, too." She took a step inside the room, hovering in the doorway. "Hey, Drew?"

"Yes?"

"I don't want to be alone tonight."

"You won't be," he murmured, straightening the teardrop pendant on her necklace. "I'll be right next door. If you need anything, just call out my name."

Her body shivered as his fingertips delicately grazed her neck. "Let me put it this way. I don't want to *sleep* alone tonight."

The pair didn't break their gaze as she backed into the bedroom. A deep sense of longing spun through Nia's core when Drew followed, closing the door behind them.

Chapter Eighteen

The rows of dark green Douglas fir trees lining Ensley Lane were all a blur as Drew navigated the winding road. He glanced over at Nia, whose pulsating temples had to be aching by now as they'd been going nonstop since the officers left the station.

"How much longer until we get to Lake Astor?" she asked for a third time.

"About fifteen minutes. Maybe a little sooner since traffic is pretty light."

Drew reached across the console and slid his hand over hers. While she didn't glance in his direction, her fingers intertwined within his. He knew she wasn't in the mood to talk. So he continued to let the smooth jazz flowing through the speakers fill the gaps of silence.

Waking up with Nia lying in his arms felt surreal after their explosive night of lovemaking. They'd poured every pent-up emotion into the moment. Drew could still feel the sensation of her supple skin lingering on his lips. He'd wanted more of her this morning. But the moment she had opened her eyes Nia was all business, anxiously anticipating their meeting with Coco.

Once they arrived at the station, she immediately began digging into the investigation. She'd followed up with

Someone for Everyone as the company had yet to submit the subpoenaed documentation. The court-imposed deadline was fast approaching, prompting Officer Ryan to look into having the app shut down until they complied.

At twelve-thirty sharp Nia charged Drew's desk, insisting that they head to Lake Astor just in case Coco decided to leave for New Mexico early. According to the navigation system, they were set to arrive almost thirty minutes earlier than the two o'clock meeting time. Drew just hoped the afternoon wouldn't lead to disappointment.

"In five hundred feet," the navigation system announced, "turn left onto Sandcastle Road. The destination will be on your right."

Nia's grasp on his hand tightened as she leaned forward, staring out the window. "We're almost there."

Within minutes, a two-story cabin deckhouse appeared in the distance. The bright afternoon sun gleamed against the floor-to-ceiling windows. Silverleaf maple trees surrounded the property's vast acreage, with a sizable lake flowing along the side of the home.

As Drew tapped the navigation screen and ended the route, Nia rapped on the window.

"What is going on out here?"

He pulled up to the house's vast front yard, then slammed on the brakes. Yellow caution tape had been wrapped around the lower deck and several nearby trees. Law enforcement officers dressed in hazmat suits were scattered across the front yard. Farther in the distance, a white sheet lay near the edge of the river.

The sight turned Drew's stomach. He peered over at Nia, whose hand covered her mouth.

"I think I'm gonna be sick," she gagged.

"Let's just stay calm," he told her, his steady tone masking the trepidation coursing through his body. "We don't know what's going on here yet."

"I think I have a pretty good idea."

Drew threw open the door and jumped out. "Let me go talk to the officers, then I'll come back and let you—"

"Absolutely not," Nia interrupted, climbing out and following him up the driveway. "I'm coming with you."

Together the pair rushed over to a group of officers. One in particular approached them with his arms in the air.

"Hey!" he shouted. "I'm gonna need for you to get back. This area is closed off."

Drew flashed his badge then extended a hand. "Sir, my name is Officer Taylor, and this is Officer Brooks. We're with the Juniper PD and were scheduled to meet with Coco Campbell here. She told us that her parents own this place."

Despite the detective's face being covered with a mask, Drew noticed his fiery glare soften. "Oh, my apologies. I'm Detective Reynolds with the Lake Astor PD. And um… yeah. I'm sorry to have to tell you this, but Ms. Campbell is dead."

"Oh my God," Nia moaned, doubling over in shock. Drew grabbed her right before she went tumbling to the ground.

"Did you two know her personally?" the detective asked.

"Not exactly," Drew told him. "I'm sure you've heard about the serial killer case we're working up in Juniper. Officer Brooks and I are the lead investigators, and Coco had some information that we were hoping might lead us to the suspect."

Detective Reynolds ran his thumbnail across his brows. "Oh boy. Welp, I wonder if the information she was planning to share has anything to do with her murder."

Nia stood straight up and pulled in a long breath of air.

"Coco was a friend of my sister's, Ivy Brooks. She's gone missing." Gesturing toward the sheet covering her body, she choked, "Who found her? And was her throat slashed?"

"A couple of deer hunters were out here early this morning and spotted the body. Judging by the looks of her swollen lips and bruising around the neck, we're thinking she died by asphyxiation. But of course the medical examiner will need to perform an autopsy to confirm that."

"So she wasn't bound at all?" Drew asked.

"No, she wasn't."

Pivoting away from the officers, Nia uttered, "That means we really could be dealing with two killers here."

A couple of men dressed in dark gray suits appeared from behind the house. Alongside them was an extremely petite woman dressed in pink pajama pants and a brown leather aviator jacket. Her shoulders shook as she sobbed uncontrollably, using her long red hair to wipe away the tears.

Detective Reynolds pointed toward the group. "You two may wanna speak with Elena. She was a friend of Coco's. They were supposed to drive down to New Mexico together today. Once she's done with the homicide detectives, I'll send her over."

The officers exchanged business cards, with Reynolds promising to reach out once the crime scene evidence came back from the lab.

As soon as the detective walked away, Nia leaned into Drew. "I have got the worst feeling that Ivy is dead."

"Don't say that. You have got to keep your head in a good space, Nia. If for nothing else, for the sake of your sister. That's the only way you're gonna get through this. We'll be hoping for the best until we can't anymore. Now let's see what this friend of Coco's has to say, all right?"

When she failed to respond, Drew reached down and lifted her chin. His chest pulled at the pain in her eyes. "You heard what Detective Reynolds said. Coco's cause of death is nothing like the other victims. Her murder may not have anything to do with this case we're working." He knew the statement was wishful thinking on his part. But Drew was desperate to say something, *anything*, to prevent Nia from falling apart.

"Hey!" Coco's friend Elena shrieked as she ran toward Drew and Nia. "You're Ivy's sister?"

"I am. You're Elena, right?"

"Yes," she whimpered before collapsing into Nia's arms.

Drew grabbed both women as they teetered back and forth. "Why don't we go sit inside the car and talk?"

"Good idea," Nia told him while they both helped a stumbling Elena across the lawn.

Once inside the vehicle, the officers pulled out their notebooks and turned to the back seat where Elena was sitting.

"I know your sister," she croaked. "Very well. We worked together for Legacy. It's like this high-society men's club. Did you, um...did you know anything about that?"

"I didn't. At least not until Ivy went missing and I read about it in her journal. What type of work do you do for the club?"

"I bartended at the meetings. Just like Ivy. But I quit and was about to move to New Mexico with Coco, until..." Her voice broke as a low groan gurgled inside her throat.

"We're so sorry for your loss," Drew said. "Can I ask why you quit the job?"

"Yeah," she sniffled, wiping her nose on the sleeve of her coat. "Because just like Ivy, I was sick of all the harassment and gross behavior. The members treated us like we were their property or something. And they were never reprimanded. We were just expected to take it. Which most of us did because the money was so good. I'm actually surprised Ivy didn't fight harder to keep her job when she was fired. She was getting paid more than most of us. But I get it. Ivy was sick of the guys asking for more than just friendly conversations and dinner dates. When she was let go, her plan was to return to Juniper and focus on her singing career."

"Is one of the guys you're referring to known as The Donor?" Nia asked.

"Yep, he's one of them. He's the main one, actually."

"Do you know his name?"

"Yeah. It's Ethan Rogers."

"What do you know about him?" Drew probed.

Biting down on her cuticles, Elena mumbled, "If I get into this, you all have got to promise me you'll keep my name out of it. Because those Legacy members are a trip. And I do not wanna end up like Coco and Iv—" She paused, her head jerking in Nia's direction. "I'm sorry. But, I mean…"

Instead of appearing solemn, there was a determination in Nia's taut expression.

"You have our word," she told Elena. "Now tell us everything you know about Ethan."

Pride erupted inside Drew's chest at her strength. In that moment, he couldn't have been prouder to have her as his partner.

"Ethan," Elena spewed. "Where should I even start. He and Ivy got really cool when she first started working for Legacy. After a while, he started buying her all these expensive gifts and paying her rent. He was there for her as a friend, too. And eventually, as a protector."

"Wait," Nia interjected. "What do you mean as a protector?"

Rolling her eyes toward the roof of the car, Elena emitted a loud snort. "Yeah, so Ivy had a fan club of sorts back in LA that included a stalkerish ex-boyfriend and an overly friendly neighbor. When she and the boyfriend broke up, he wouldn't leave her alone. He kept popping up at her apartment, begging her to take him back. He'd call and text nonstop. Leave flowers and love letters at her front door. She'd made it clear that there wasn't a chance in hell they'd rekindle the relationship. But the man just wouldn't give up."

Drew paused his note-taking and turned to Nia. "Did you know about any of this?"

"No, I didn't. I hadn't read about any of it in Ivy's journal, either." She nodded in Elena's direction. "Sorry, go on."

"Yeah, so as for Ivy's incel of a neighbor…*whew.* That weirdo would magically appear everywhere she went. The grocery store, the gym, her singing gigs. Eventually it got to be too much, and she told Ethan what was going on with both guys. I don't know what that man did. But soon after she talked to him, the harassment just stopped. The next time Ivy saw Ethan, he told her that she wouldn't have to worry about either of the guys ever again."

Both Drew and Nia sat there, neither wanting to ask the inevitable. Several moments passed before Drew finally spoke up.

"What, uh…what exactly do you think Ethan did to the men?"

"Either he beat their asses or threatened to. Because after that, whenever Ivy ran into the neighbor, he'd barely speak, duck his head and keep it moving. As for the ex-boyfriend, he ended up moving to Florida to live with his brother."

"Hmph," Nia sighed. "Well, I'm glad to hear he didn't

kill them. But wait, if Ethan was looking out for Ivy and doing all these nice things for her, why did they fall out?"

"Because the more he did, the more he expected. Ivy was content with just being friends. Ethan wasn't. Over time, his feelings for her grew into some sort of twisted infatuation. It became dark. And menacing. I'm telling you, the man was obsessed."

"Do you think he has anything to do with Ivy going missing?"

Elena paused, twisting her hands together as tears welled in her eyes. "I do."

Piercing silence filled the car. Drew's pen stopped in the middle of the page before he expanded the probe, asking, "What about Coco's murder? Do you think he's involved in that as well?"

"I do. Because just like Ivy, she knew too much."

"What did she know?"

"I'm not exactly sure. But it had something to do with him and another club member named Vaughn Clayton. Vaughn is a big-time attorney who's running for senator here in Colorado, and Ethan is the head of his fundraising committee. If you ask me, everything about their partnership is shady. And I think Ivy and Coco discovered a few things that the men didn't want to be known. Exactly what I don't know. But that's just my two cents."

"Are you still in touch with anyone who works for Legacy?" Nia questioned.

"*Hell* no. None of those bitches deserve my friendship. I was so good to all of them. But when I needed backup after complaining to our manager about the way I was being hassled, nobody had my back. They all turned on me. They're all about the money. I'm not surprised though. Those girls have yet to learn that all money isn't good money."

Slamming her notebook shut, Nia thanked Elena for the information, then nudged Drew's arm. "We need to find this Ethan guy and have a talk with him."

"I agree. Why don't we head back to the station and figure out where to—"

"I know where you can find him," Elena interrupted.

"Where?"

"At the next Legacy meeting."

"Do you know when and where it'll be?" Drew replied skeptically. "You know, since you no longer work for the club or speak to your ex-colleagues."

"I still have a couple of connections within the club. I heard that the guys are getting together this Friday night at Richard's Cigar Lounge in downtown Denver. The meeting starts at eight o'clock sharp."

Nia tore her notebook open and wrote down the information. "Good to know. Thank you."

"Oh, and there's one more thing you should know," Elena said.

"What's that?"

"Ethan Rogers sometimes goes by another name. He claims it's for business purposes. But I think there's more to it than that."

Pausing his pen, Drew's eyes drifted from his notebook to Elena. "Oh, really? What's the other name?"

"Shane Anderson."

Chapter Nineteen

"9-1-1. What is your emergency?"

Nia turned up the volume on her phone and held her breath, shivering as the night breeze blew past her. Crouching down behind a row of perfectly manicured boxwood shrubs, she took another look around the vast backyard.

"Hello, 9-1-1," the operator repeated. "Do you need police, fire or medical?"

"I need the police," Nia hissed, barely able to force the words from her constricting throat.

She craned her neck. Stared out toward the massive white pines lining the back of the yard. That shadowy figure she'd just seen darting through the pruned tree trunks was nowhere in sight. Neither was Drew, who should've been there by now.

Juniper PD's plan to raid the Legacy club meeting at the cigar lounge had gone completely awry. And Nia had no one to blame but herself. She was the one who'd insisted that Ethan, also known as Shane, was the only person who could lead them to Ivy. If they confronted him at Richard's, she feared they'd never find her sister. So she insisted they hold off and follow him after the meeting.

Once Ethan and Vaughn left the lounge together, law enforcement trailed the men to the house on Webb Hill

Road. Unbeknownst to Nia, who had driven her own car from Juniper to Denver, she'd been the first officer to arrive on the scene. A flickering bulb hanging over the coach house's porch had caught her attention. She'd sent Drew a text letting him know she would meet him there.

Desperately hoping to get to her sister, Nia exited her vehicle and began casing the house's exterior. At one point she could've sworn she'd seen Drew hovering near the coach house doorway, signaling her over. But as she got closer, Nia realized the short, stocky figure dressed in all black was not him.

As she approached, the man lunged at her. She panicked, freezing underneath the grip of his strong, massive hands. Everything happened so fast that Nia didn't have time to draw her weapon. A brief tussle ensued. She'd managed to land a right hook, then slip from his grasp, only to roll her ankle while running to safety.

"I'm sorry, ma'am," the operator said, jolting Nia from her thoughts. "Could you please repeat that? And speak up a bit, if possible?"

"I. Need. *Help!*"

She fell to her knees, her feet aching and head pounding simultaneously.

"What is your location?"

"Forty-two Webb Hill Road."

"Can you tell me what's going on there?"

Covering her mouth, Nia whispered, "I've been attacked. I was able to get away, and now I'm hiding in the backyard. The assailant is still out there somewhere. I'm a Juniper police officer and my team was supposed to meet me here, but we got separated. So now I'm alone, it's pitch-black and I can hardly see a thing."

Frustration stiffened Nia's limbs. She stared up at the

gloomy, cloudless sky. Only a few dim streams of light beamed from the scattered stars. They did nothing to break through the relentless darkness blanketing the yard.

"I've got law enforcement heading your way. What is your name, ma'am?"

"Officer Brooks. Officer Nia Brooks—"

Bang! Bang!

"Hello? Officer Brooks? Were those gunshots I just heard?"

"Yes!" Nia screeched into the phone.

"Were you struck?"

"I…no, but I—"

Bang!

Nia hit the ground, narrowly dodging the bullet that flew over her head. A scream threatened to escape her lips. But she bit down on her jaw, knowing one wrong move could end her life.

"Listen to me, Officer Brooks. I'm going to need for you to take cover and stay on the line with me. Denver PD is already en route, okay?"

"Okay. *Please* tell them to hurry."

Blades of grass cut into Nia's cheek as she inhaled the damp, earthy dirt. She thought back on her days of working as a 9-1-1 operator. Being on the other side of danger felt surreal. This moment was eerily similar to the night she'd received the call from Linda Echols. With one exception—Nia was armed.

She unholstered her Glock 22 and squeezed the grip, bracing herself for another round of gunfire.

"Officer Brooks, my name is Sydney. I'll be right here on the line with you until police arrive, all right?"

"Yes, thank you, Sydney." Nia clutched her throbbing ankle, peeking through the bushes as her attacker sprinted across the back of the yard. "How much longer until they'll be here?"

"Just a few more minutes. Hang in there."

A sobering thought crossed Nia's mind—Drew still wasn't there. She wondered if they'd crossed paths with Denver's police department. "Has anyone in your department heard from the Juniper PD?"

"Not as far as I know. But I'll send out a message to dispatch and find out. In the meantime, have you spotted the shooter again?"

"I think I see him lurking in the wooded area behind the backyard. But I'm not sure. I've got my weapon drawn and I'm ready to shoot if necess—"

Boom!

"Officer Brooks! Are shots being fired again?"

The phone went silent.

"Officer Brooks, talk to me. Are you okay?"

"Yes," Nia finally uttered through shallow breaths.

Just as another round of shots rang out, someone yelled in the distance, "Officer Brooks! Where are you?"

"Drew!" Nia screamed.

The sound of his voice eased the tension coursing through her body. She hopped to her knees, peering through the bushes while waving an arm in the air. "I'm over—"

Bang!

A bullet ricocheted right past her shoulder.

"Stay down, Brooks!" Drew yelled. "The other officers are surrounding the premises—"

Boom!

Drew's voice faded as a loud thud echoed through the air.

"Officer Taylor?" Nia shouted. "Officer Taylor!"

Another bullet flew past her ear. She burrowed deep

within the grass, gripping her chest after what sounded like a body dropping to the ground.

Sirens blared right before footsteps pounded the winding driveway's pavement.

"Police! Drop your weapon and come out with your hands up!"

Nia recognized the voice. It was Chief Mitchell.

"Officer Brooks," Sydney said into the phone, "I'm still here with you. It sounds like the police are on the scene."

"Yes, they're here," she moaned, her tone flattened by the thought of Drew being shot.

I've got to get to him...

Nia slid to her knees. Curled her finger around the trigger while glaring through the brush. The officers' darting flashlights spilled across the lawn. She scanned the yard for the shooter as an urge to call out Drew's name singed her tongue.

Don't do it...

"We need paramedics at forty-two Webb Hill Road!" Sydney yelled through the phone. *"Stat!"*

Dread pricked Nia's skin. An ambulance was probably being called to the scene for Drew.

You cannot let this man die...

Her eyes burned with determination just as she caught sight of the black-clad husky figure she'd seen earlier, creeping toward a sloped rock garden. He hid behind a boulder, then shot at the officers.

"Take cover!" Chief Mitchell commanded.

Nia took aim. Fired one bullet. The shooter fell onto his back.

"We got him!" someone yelled before law enforcement charged the attacker.

Jumping up and running in the opposite direction, Nia's legs went numb right before she crumpled to the ground.

Get on your feet! a voice screamed inside her head.

She dug her palms into the ground, steadied herself and stood, then pressed on in search of Drew.

"Officer Brooks?" Sydney asked. "Are you still there?"

"I am," she panted into the phone. "But I need to hang up and check on my partner."

"Understood. Good luck, Officer."

Disconnecting the call, Nia stayed low while charging across the backyard.

"Drew!" she screamed, spinning in circles while frantically searching the grounds.

Her vision blurred with fear as she peered through the darkness. Chaos reeled all around her. Law enforcement darted in between the trees and bushes. Flashlights beamed in every direction. Gunshots intent on taking down each officer in the vicinity were firing at every moving target.

"Take cover!" Chief Mitchell yelled. "And don't shoot unless you've got a clear shot!"

Ignoring the directive, Nia kept moving, stumbling through the thick patches of grass. Another round of bullets whizzed through the air. She wanted to stop but couldn't. Not until she found Drew.

"Nia! Over here!"

"Drew!"

She sped toward him, almost falling to the ground before collapsing into his arms. "I thought you were—"

"Don't even say it. I'm fine. Now we've got to stay focused. I just saw Ethan and Vaughn run inside the house. I'm gonna have Officer Davis bang on the front door while we force our way in through the back." He paused, staring out at the lawn. "After the way those guys came at us with their guns blazing, I have no doubt they're hiding something in there."

Trembling at the thought of her sister being found dead, Nia stared at Drew, searching his tense expression for a glint of hope. Their eyes met. He pulled her close, the energy flowing within his embrace filling her with reassurance—as if he knew what she needed without having to be told.

For a brief moment, Nia thought about their night together. They'd been so wrapped up in finding Ivy that they had yet to discuss it. But what was understood didn't need to be explained. She knew the opportunity to express their feelings would soon come. In this moment, however, their only goal was to get her sister back.

"It's time to move in!" Chief Mitchell yelled.

As he directed several officers toward the front of the house, Drew shot the lock off the back door. He kicked his way inside with Nia following closely behind, staying low while spreading out inside the dark dining room.

"Police!" he yelled. "Whoever's in here needs to make themselves known. Come out with your hands above your head!"

Nia flinched at the sound of Officer Davis's fist pounding the front door, then fell to the floor when bullets came rushing past them.

Drew grabbed her arm and pulled her behind a stately oak hutch.

"Take cover!" he warned law enforcement as they bumrushed the living room.

Tightening the straps on her bulletproof vest, Nia rose to her feet.

"There's no one in my line of vision," she whispered,

pressing her head against the back of the unit while glancing around the corner.

"Same here. I'm trying to figure out where the shots are coming from."

Officer Davis threw a hand in the air, signaling toward the staircase. Drew gave him a thumbs-up, then placed his hand over his head, indicating he'd cover him.

Just as the officer made a move, a blast of bullets flashed once more.

"The assailant is to the right of the stairs!" Nia shouted.

Together, she and Drew fired back while Officers Davis and Ryan slid underneath the dining table. Glass shattered over their heads as slivers of champagne flutes crashed to the floor. For a brief moment, both sides ceased fire. But the echo of bullets still rang through the air.

"There's another shooter upstairs!" Drew warned.

Nia stooped down, checking to make sure the other officers hadn't been hit. They each nodded before raising their weapons.

"Ethan and Vaughn must have split up," she told Drew. "One is covering the front door while the other is covering the back—" She stopped at the sound of Officer Mills's voice.

"Get down on the floor! Hands over your head. Now!"

An audible gasp came from the room to the right of the staircase, followed by the loud thump of metal hitting the floor. Nia's arms trembled as adrenaline ripped through her body. Repositioning her gun, she pointed it toward the doorway, hoping the shooter would appear.

Drew stepped around Nia and threw the other officers a signal. "That was the shooter's magazine. He's out of bullets. Let's move in!"

He led the squad toward the room just as a man appeared in the doorway.

"Drop your weapon!" Drew yelled. "Get those hands in the air!"

As the officers swooped in, Nia froze. Faint screams filled the gaps of chaos circling around her. She turned her ear in the direction of the pleas. Through the darkness, she was able to make out a door near the back of the dining room.

She darted toward it. Reached for the knob. When the door failed to open, Nia ran her hands along the frame. A metal bolt scraped at her palm. She rammed it to the side and yanked at the door once more. The second it cracked open, a dark figure appeared from behind a curtain hanging from the dining room's windows.

"Dre—" Nia called out right before a gloved hand covered her mouth. The bitter taste of leather grazed her tongue. In one fell swoop she was pulled behind the curtain and knocked to the floor.

Nia's gun fell from her hand and slid across the hardwood planks. She threw an elbow, jabbing her attacker in his side. A chilling grunt rumbled from his mouth.

"You *bitch*," was all she heard before his hand slid from her mouth to her throat.

"Drew..." Nia wheezed, his name dissolving in the air as pressure crushed her neck.

Kicking out at her attacker, she struggled to make contact. But he slid from side to side, making it impossible to land a blow.

Nia's eyes rolled into the back of her head. Shallow streams of breath seeped through her quivering lips. She reached out, her hand shaking as she tried to hit the floor. Grab Drew's attention. Tell him she was in danger.

"Die, bitch," the man rasped. *"Die!"*

Drew... Nia screamed in her mind as the word couldn't escape through her constricting lungs. She struggled to see through the darkness. To catch a glimpse of her attacker. A sheet of sweat covered her face as her body went limp. Everything around her grew hazy, then blackened. A dizzying spell filled her head as she felt herself fading.

"Nia!"

Footsteps pounded the floor as the sound of Drew's voice brought her to. The grip on her neck loosened, then released.

Boom!

A kick to the gut from Drew's boot sent her attacker rolling across the floor. Officer Ryan swooped in and pounced, subduing then handcuffing who she now realized was Ethan.

Blinking rapidly, Nia slowly sat up and clutched her throat. Willed herself to regroup. And find Ivy.

"Nia!" Drew panted, pulling the officer to her feet. "Are you all right? Ethan... He just—he came out of nowhere. And I thought you were right behind me. I should've kept a better eye on you. I am so sorry!"

"It's okay," she gasped. "I'm fine. I just need to get my bearings—"

Faint screams came from the lower level.

"Ivy," Nia said. "I think I hear Ivy!"

Drew held her up as she stumbled toward the door. Throwing it open, Nia screamed out her sister's name.

"I'm down here! In the basement!"

Taking the stairs two at a time, Nia practically skied through the darkness. "Ivy! I don't see you. Keep talking!"

"Hold on, Nia!" Drew called out, pulling her back. "Where's your gun?"

She pressed her hands against her body before pointing toward the ceiling. "*Dammit*. I dropped it when I was being attacked."

He drew his weapon and covered her. "Stay close and let me lead the way. We don't know who may be lurking around down here."

Hovering near Drew's side, Nia called out Ivy's name once again. "Make some noise, Ivy! Where are you?"

"In here!" she yelled as the sound of banging rang out.

Nia ran her hands along the wall in a frantic search for a light switch. "I can hardly see a thing. Drew, *help*!"

Within seconds, the room lit up. Nia looked over and saw him standing across the way, gripping a metal pull string hanging from a lightbulb.

"*Thank* you," she uttered while eyeing their strange surroundings.

Sheets of plastic dangled from the ceiling, their edges crumpled against the dusty floor. Exposed wood and insulation lined the unfinished walls. The few pieces of furniture scattered around the spacious area were covered in paint-splattered drop cloths.

"*Nia!*"

The sound of Ivy's voice sent the officers rushing toward a back corner. A thick, dirty canvas tarp hung across the wall. Nia yanked it to the floor, revealing a narrow wooden door. It was secured shut with an alloy steel padlock.

"Ivy, stand back!" Nia yelled. "Step away from the door!"

Drew took aim and blew off the lock, then kicked down the door.

"*Ivy!*" Nia screamed, rushing inside. Relief rattled her chest when her sister appeared inside the dimly lit makeshift bedroom.

Stumbling around a gray chest of drawers, Ivy fell into her arms.

"Thank God you found me," she sobbed.

Holding her as tight as she could, Nia said, "Of course we found you. But…how did this happen? How did you get here?"

A guttural moan vibrated against Nia's shoulder as Ivy's body wracked in agony. "I was getting ready to go to the sound check at Army and Lou's, and there was a knock at the door. I thought it was Madison, there to give me a ride during her break at Bullseye. I didn't even look through the peephole before opening the door. When I did, Ethan was standing on the other side. I just knew he was gonna kill me right there on the spot and freaked out. The second I screamed, he attacked, covering my mouth and pushing me back inside the apartment. All I remember is the sting of a needle being jabbed into my arm. When I woke up, I was inside this tiny hellhole."

Nia was overcome by a flood of emotions as she held her sister tighter. "Well, we're here now. I'm just so glad we got to you in time, before…" Her voice broke. She couldn't bring herself to say the words *before he killed you*.

The thought of Coco sprang to mind. Nia couldn't tell Ivy what had happened to her, either. At least not yet.

Tramping overhead alerted the officers that there was still work to be done. Holding on to Nia's shoulder, Drew said, "Keep your sister safe," before turning to Ivy. "We're so glad you're okay. Once we secure this place, we'll get you to the hospital. In the meantime, we need to arrest these bastards."

Chapter Twenty

Drew and Nia entered Chief Mitchell's office, neither of them able to wipe the smiles off their faces.

"Welcome back, Chief. How are you feeling?" Drew asked, pointing at the sling cradling his boss's left arm. During the shootout Chief Mitchell had been hit in the shoulder, landing him in the hospital for a couple of days, then at home for over a week.

"I'm feeling pretty good thanks to a little time off and eight hundred milligrams of ibuprofen every six hours. What've you two got for me?"

"A lot," Drew replied, sliding a copy of the case file across the desk. "Have you been keeping up with the reports we've emailed to you?"

The chief sat straight up and flipped open the file. "I have. But I wanna hear everything I've missed direct from you two. So have a seat and fill me in."

Raising her hand in the air, Nia said, "Wait, before we get started, can I just share with you that my phone, along with Officer Taylor's, has been ringing off the hook ever since Ethan and Vaughn were arrested?"

"And you're not alone in that," Chief Mitchell replied, chuckling into his coffee mug before taking a long sip. "I think every member of this community has called singing the department's praises. It's safe to say they're all breathing easier these days, thanks to you two. But anyway, let's get to it. Give me a rundown of the interrogations."

"So," Drew began, "as you can probably guess, both men turned on one another the second they started talking. Ethan claimed that Vaughn had been misappropriating the funds he'd donated to his senatorial campaign to bankroll his lavish lifestyle, then accused him of being Juniper's serial killer after he'd had multiple affairs with the murdered women."

"Did he mention what his motive would've been?"

"He did. According to Ethan, Vaughn was worried that the women would leak details of their liaisons and ruin his political career."

"*And* his marriage," Nia added. "But as for Ivy's friend Coco, Ethan alleged Vaughn killed her because she knew about the misused funds. He was afraid she'd blow the whistle."

"What about Ivy?" Chief Mitchell asked. "Vaughn wasn't worried about how much she knew?"

"He was. According to Ethan, Vaughn wanted her dead, too. But Ethan wouldn't allow it, and claims he was keeping her safe at his house so that Vaughn couldn't get to her."

The chief reached across the desk and switched on the fan. "So what did Vaughn have to say for himself?"

"Brace yourself," Drew responded, flipping through his copy of the report. "Because Vaughn presented a completely different side to this sadistic story. Officer Brooks and I started off light. We questioned him about the whole misappropriated campaign funds situation first. He claimed that Ethan was the one who'd misused the money by making illegal donations in hopes of influencing policies that would benefit his businesses."

"Then," Nia interjected, "without being prompted, Vaughn went straight to the murders. He called Ethan a possessive, controlling sociopath who met each of the victims through Someone for Everyone and killed them after they broke things off with him. And according to him, Ethan actually *owns* the dating app."

"A fact that he kept hidden after registering the company as an anonymous limited liability," Drew said.

"Hmph," Chief Mitchell huffed. "Sounds to me like both of these men could've had a hand in all this."

Shifting in her chair, Nia said, "Well, just to add another odd layer to an already twisted story, I actually connected with Ethan through Someone for Everyone. During Vaughn's interrogation, he claimed that since Ethan had been rejected by Ivy, he went after the next best thing."

"Meaning…you?"

"Yes. Exactly. But the night we were supposed to meet up, he was a no-show. Ethan felt as though he'd be betraying Ivy by going out with me. Then when he found out I was one of the lead investigators working the serial killer case, Vaughn claimed that it was Ethan who began stalking and harassing me in hopes of disrupting the investigation."

"Wow," Chief Mitchel grunted. "And the plot thickens…"

Drew threw Nia a look, then slid another report across the table. "Let's get to the good stuff, shall we?"

"What is this?" the chief asked.

"A present from the forensic lab. They processed the evidence in record time and we've already got the results back."

"And?" Chief Mitchell boomed through a widening grin.

"Ethan's DNA matched the evidence collected at the crime scenes of Katie Douglas, Violet Shields and Ingrid

Porter. Those footprint impressions Officer Brooks discovered at Katie's and Violet's crime scenes matched a pair of size eleven Lacrosse AeroHead Sport hunting boots that we took from Ethan's house. Blood evidence found on the soles matched both victims' DNA."

"Good work, Brooks."

"Thank you, sir."

"What about Vaughn? Anything come back on him?"

"Oh, yeah," Nia said. "His DNA matched perspiratory evidence found on the body of Coco Campbell. That gave credence to Ethan's claim that she was aware of the illegalities involving Vaughn's campaign, prompting him to kill her before she could expose his illicit campaign activity. *And...*" Nia pivoted in her seat, giving Drew's shoulder a nudge. "I'll let Drew share the rest."

Chief Mitchell looked up from the report. "Go on. I'm listening."

"So, once Ethan's DNA was entered in the criminal database, one of our department's cold cases was cracked. Remember Linda Echols?"

"Of course. How could I forget?"

"Well, the nightgown Linda was wearing the evening she was murdered contained Ethan's DNA. After speaking with her sister, I found out Linda was a member of Someone for Everyone at the time of her death. We didn't figure that out earlier because she used a fake name on the app."

Pounding his fist onto the desk, the chief rocked against the back of his chair and stared up at the ceiling. "This is the best news I've gotten all year! See, I knew it. I knew you two would somehow get that case solved, too." He shot back up and pointed at Drew. "Aren't you glad that I—"

"Yes," Drew interrupted before Chief Mitchell could finish his statement. "I am *ecstatic* that you insisted I team up with Officer Brooks. Now let's get back to the case before things start getting mushy around here. I still believe that either Ethan or Vaughn caused Tim's car accident due to his involvement in this investigation. But before you even say it, I already know that charge can't be filed since I have no supporting evidence. Nevertheless, I'd be remiss if I didn't at least bring it up."

"Well, we'll continue to keep an eye out. If some sort of evidence does emerge, then we'll file charges. What's the status of the third suspect involved in the shootout?"

"Turns out he was a private security guard hired by Ethan to patrol his home. He's the one who attacked Nia when she first arrived on the scene."

"What's his status?"

"Still in the hospital in critical but stable condition."

Running a hand over his injured shoulder, Chief Mitchell replied, "And once he's discharged he'll go straight to prison. On another note, how did your call go with the district attorney?"

"Great," Drew told him. "She's planning on charging Ethan with four counts of first-degree murder, aggravated kidnapping, attempted murder and conspiracy. Vaughn's being charged first-degree murder, conspiracy, and aiding and abetting. In the meantime, both men are being held without bond."

"Oh, that is *awe*—" The chief groaned, wincing while gripping his shoulder.

"Are you okay?" Nia asked just as his cell phone rang.

"Ugh, I will be. I guess I should've listened to my wife when she told me to stay home a few more days to recuperate. But how could I when all this excitement was happening around here?" He glanced down at the phone. "Speaking of my wife, I'd better grab her call. I'll circle back with you both this afternoon. Thanks again for the great work on this investigation."

"You're welcome, sir."

As Drew followed Nia out of the office, his eyes drifted down to her hips. He shoved his hands inside his pockets, reminding himself that it wouldn't be appropriate to wrap her up in his arms in front of the entire department. Yet in that moment, he felt so full. Emotion was churning inside his chest. With Nia by his side, the pair had managed to solve one of the biggest cases in Juniper's history.

In the midst of it all, memories of their steamy evening together occupied his mind more often than he'd like to admit. As the case continued to heat up, however, there hadn't been time to address that night and talk about whether either of them wanted more.

But now that Ethan and Vaughn were finally behind bars, Drew planned on sitting down with Nia and putting it all on the table, sooner rather than later.

Epilogue

One month later...

Nia pressed her hand against her chest as she approached the door to Army and Lou's. Peering through the frosted glass, she could already tell that she was overdressed. Most patrons were wearing jeans and button-down shirts, or leggings and oversized sweaters. Nia must have missed the memo. She'd chosen a mini tuxedo dress, which she thought would be appropriate since the Juniper PD was gathering to celebrate Drew's promotion to detective.

The moment she stepped inside the club, all eyes were on her. Nia greeted everyone through a stiff smile, squeezing past the crowd of people lining the hallway. She focused on the photos hanging from the wall rather than the ogling expressions on clubgoers' faces.

A loud, familiar roar of laughter echoed from the back of the main room, signaling that her colleagues were gathered near the stage. As she headed that way, a waving hand caught her attention over by the bar.

"Hey, Officer Brooks!"

Nia waved back while Officer Ryan made his way toward her.

"Wow," he uttered, eyeing her from head to toe. "You

look…*fantastic*. I don't think I've ever seen you all dressed up like this. Wait, are those real diamonds on your shoes?"

"I wish," she said, laughing as the officer offered her his arm.

"This place is packed tonight," he said. "I'll escort you to the spot where the manager roped off a section for us."

"Thanks, Officer Ryan."

Nia teetered on her heels, struggling not to bump into anyone on the way to their section. The atmosphere was electric as strobe lights shone down on a quartet playing a rendition of Dizzy Gillespie's "Get Happy." The dance floor was packed with couples swinging to the rhythm of the music. And almost everyone there looked to have a drink in their hand and a smile on their face.

Several officers greeted Nia as she approached. While responding with enthusiastic hellos, there was only one thing on her mind—finding Drew.

Her heart stuttered the moment she laid eyes on him. He looked up, as if he could feel her presence. Nia's lips curled into a soft smile. Unlike the other officers, Drew had dressed up, appearing so handsome in his slim-fitting beige suit and crisp white shirt. He tossed her a sexy head nod while his eyes roamed her body. They paused on her arm, which was still nestled within Officer Ryan's. The grin on Drew's face quickly shriveled in a confused scowl.

"We've got a ton of food set up here," the officer told Nia, motioning toward platters filled with buffalo wings, pepperoni flatbread and Philly cheesesteak sliders. "And there's wine, champagne, and of course, beer. If you want a craft cocktail, you'll have to order that at the bar. Or I'd be happy to go over and grab something for you. Anything you want. Just say the word."

Nia's skin prickled as he leaned in closer. She slipped her arm out of his grip and said, "Thanks, but I'm fine for now."

When she walked over to the table and poured herself a glass of ice water, he followed.

"You know," he began, swinging his mug of beer toward the dance floor, "I love this song. Would you like to—"

"Hey, Ryan!" someone called out behind them. "Why don't you at least let Officer Brooks settle in before you try and make a move on her?"

Nia didn't have to turn around to know that it was Drew.

Raising his hands in surrender, Officer Ryan replied, "It isn't even like that. I was just being friendly. No need to get testy, *Detective Taylor.*"

"Ooh, I like the sound of that," Drew retorted. "Thanks, *Officer Ryan.*"

Drew wrapped his arm around Nia's waist and led her to a quiet corner. "Damn, that man wasn't even trying to hide the fact that he's got a crush on you."

"Give him a break. He's a nice guy."

Nia's limbs tingled with nerves as several of their colleagues eyed them curiously. But that wasn't the only reason she was feeling anxious. She had yet to talk to Drew about their intimate night together. There hadn't been much time for personal matters. Soon after the killers were arrested, Drew was hit with the news of his promotion. Adjusting to the position and heftier workload practically took over his life. Nia, however, could no longer suppress the things she needed to get off her chest.

Suddenly, the room felt excruciatingly warm. She almost choked on the thick, steamy air circulating around them. Taking a long sip of water, Nia fanned her face before setting the glass down.

"What's going on?" Drew asked. "Are you okay?"

"I, um…" she said right before her cell phone buzzed.

"Let me guess. That's your sister texting you."

Nia smiled and showed him the message. "Of course that's Ivy texting me."

Hey big sis! Just checking in, as you've insisted I do every minute of the day. My audition for I Made It to Broadway is tomorrow morning so I'm heading to bed. Wish me luck!

"Nice," Drew responded. "Tell her I said good luck, too. How's her move back to LA going?"

"Good. Really good. She's happy to be back out there working on her craft."

"Glad to hear it." Drew moved in closer, taking Nia's hand in his. "Can I just say that you look absolutely stunning tonight?"

"Thank you. Listen…" She hesitated, distracted by everything going on around them. After glancing over her shoulder to make sure no one was within earshot, she continued. "There's something I need to tell you—"

"Wait," he interrupted. "You must have forgotten that tonight is my big night. Shouldn't you be holding a glass of champagne in celebration of my promotion?"

"Yes, I should be. But…"

"But what?"

"I can't."

"Why not?"

Nia stared into his inquisitive eyes as perspiration dotted her forehead. "That's what I wanted to talk to you about."

"Uh-oh. You're starting to scare me. What's going on?"

She reached out, straightening his lapel before resting her hand against his chest. "I'm pregnant."

Drew's pecs stiffened against her palm as his eyelids

fluttered in confusion. "I'm sorry. It's so loud in here. I actually thought you said that you're *pregnant*."

"I did. I am pregnant."

"Wait," he uttered, taking a step back. "Are you…are you serious?"

"I am."

Between his long pause and twitching eyelids, she didn't know what to make of his reaction.

"Nia, please don't play with my emotions like this."

"I wouldn't do that. I'm being totally serious. But your response is starting to scare me. Could you say something? *Anything?* Are you happy? Is this good news? Or…"

A wide grin covered his face.

"Of course this is good news!" he yelled, sweeping Nia off her feet and twirling her around. "Baby," Drew continued, lowering his voice. "We're gonna have a *baby*?"

"Yes. *Yes!*"

She held his face in her hands as their lips met, sealing the sweet moment with a tender kiss.

"Thank you, everyone!" the bandleader boomed into the microphone. "The Jazzets and I are gonna take a brief break while I turn the mic over to one of Juniper's finest, Chief Bruce Mitchell. Take it away, Chief."

Nia slowly pulled away from Drew. "Maybe we should go back over. I have a feeling our boss might be looking for you considering you're the man of the hour and all."

"Maybe we should. And if he calls me up, I'll try my best not to share the most thrilling news I've ever received before in my life with everyone here."

"Oh, *please* try your best not to do that!"

"I promise I won't." Drew held her chin in his hands, gently kissing her one last time before they returned to the group.

Chief Mitchell grabbed the mic and waved at the crowd. "Thank you, Evan. Hey, Detective Taylor, would you mind joining me up here?"

Nia looked on proudly while Drew headed to the stage, clapping the loudest among their cheering colleagues.

"Hey," Cynthia muttered in her ear. "What was that all about?"

"What was what all about?"

"Don't play coy with me. You know what I'm talking about! I saw you and Drew standing over in the corner all hugged up, making googly eyes at each other and whatnot."

"We'll talk about it later," Nia told her without taking her eyes off the stage.

"Yeah, okay. Just know that you *will* be spilling the tea as soon as Chief Mitchell is done with his speech."

The chief held his hands in the air to quiet the crowd. "Detective Taylor, on behalf of myself and the rest of Juniper PD, I would like to congratulate you on your promotion to detective. This well-deserved position is a testament to the outstanding work you've done for the department. Not only are you an excellent investigator, but you are a leader and the prototype of what anyone working in law enforcement should strive to be. We're all lucky to have you on the force, and for many of us, even luckier to call you a friend. Thank you for all that you've done, and most importantly, for spearheading Juniper's serial killer investigation."

Applause rippled through the room as Drew stepped to the mic, nodding humbly. "Thank you so much for those kind words, Chief Mitchell. I don't know if I've earned all that praise just yet, but hey, you're the boss, right? So far be it from me to disagree."

As the crowd broke into laughter, Drew's gaze drifted to Nia.

Oh no, she thought, that intense look in his eyes screaming *Join me onstage*.

"But seriously," Drew continued, "I certainly didn't solve the biggest case of my career alone. I had the help of this entire department. We were like a fine-tuned machine—everyone played their part. There was, however, one person who stood out from the rest."

Everyone turned to Nia. She crossed her arms over her chest, squeezing tightly while wishing the floor would open up and swallow her. Being the center of attention had never been her thing.

Cynthia reached over and uncrossed her arms. "Hey, relax. This is your moment, too. And you deserve it just as much as Detective Taylor. So enjoy it."

Sucking in a swift breath of air, Nia stood taller and shook out her arms. "You're right," she whispered, bracing herself as Drew proceeded.

"Some time ago, Chief Mitchell decided to implement a mentorship program within the department. I had just been assigned to this case and didn't think I'd have the time nor the patience to serve as a mentor. But the chief insisted, and as you know, what he says goes. So here I was, stuck with mentoring Officer Brooks."

The crowd burst into laughter while Drew's shining eyes homed in on Nia, as if she were the only person in the room.

"Then my partner and good friend, Officer Timothy Braxton, got into a terrible car accident. Thank God he made it out alive and is doing well. But back then, while I was concerned with his injuries and overwhelmed with the investigation, Officer Brooks and I were forced together on a deeper level as we worked to solve the case." Drew paused, then held out his hand. "Officer Brooks, would you please join me onstage?"

Loud clapping rattled her eardrums. She remained frozen in her stance, holding her breath while her colleagues chanted her name.

"Nia," Cynthia hissed, giving her a nudge, "get up on that stage and celebrate your accolades, girl!"

Wringing her hands together, she prayed her stilettos would hold her up as she wobbled toward Drew. He took a step down and extended his arm, then led her to the mic.

"Officer Brooks, it goes without saying that this case would not have been solved without you."

"Well, I don't know about all that, but—"

"No, it's true. I'm just glad that I didn't push back *too* hard. Because I wouldn't have realized that I'd been handed the perfect partner." He paused, slipping his hand along the small of her back. "Or gotten the chance to fall in love with you."

Rippling cheers rolled through the entire club. But Nia barely heard them. And when Drew leaned in and kissed her in front of everyone, she didn't care that all eyes were on them.

The moment their lips separated, she murmured, "I'm in love with you, too."

Nia wasn't sure whether he'd heard it. But judging by the beat of his pounding heart, she was certain that he'd felt it.

* * * * *

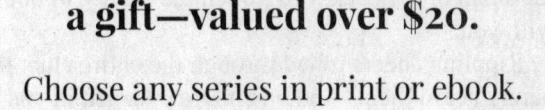